DEDICATION

To all those that supported me and helped me publish.

The Islanders Series: Green Beginnings

Drew H. Justis

Copyright © 2019 Drew H. Justis

ISBN: 1539808440

ISBN-13: 978-1539808442

ACKNOWLEDGMENTS

thanks to the vertigomaster for the cover.

Drew H. Justis

Chapter 1
Graduation
Conner

12/26/1438

Looking in the mirror I straighten my brown colored hair with my hand. Looking into my dark green eyes I smile at my reflection. Hearing a knock I look to the side and see my friend Marcus standing in the doorway. Taking a moment to admire the Combined Arms uniform I look over the dark green trousers and jacket. The uniform was simple in appearance but had several sheets of metal that protected vital organs while not hindering movement.

Marcus gives me a mock salute as he walks in and shakes my hand.
"Still can't believe we're finally done." I nod as I head over to where i'd left the box containing my own hat.
"I find it harder to believe it's only been a year." Taking out the hat I rub my thumb over the brass gun and sword that stood for the Combined Arms.
"I know what you mean. Seems like decades have gone by since we could do whatever we wanted."

I smile as I put on my hat. CA training was a year of constant training. twenty hours a day were dedicated to acquiring the skills we would need to protect king and island. It gave little free time and what little we had was spent sleeping. Turning to Marcus I tap the brim of my hat.
"We should get to our seats." Marcus nods his head and

steps behind me as I walk through the door into the hall. Once outside I see the rest of the graduating year. Not many of us left but still just over a hundred of our thousand strong class managed to get to the finish line.

Mixing with the crowd we made our way through the barracks that have served as our home for the last year of our lives. After a bit we make it to the courtyard. It was strange to see it without any targets or obstacle course. instead the whole area was covered in chairs on the far end by the gates that lead to the outside world was a simple platform with a podium.

Making my way to the front of the rows of chairs I find my seat. On my right sits Marcus and we begin talking about where we might be deployed.
"Tradition dictates we'll get put on a pirate hunter for a tour before getting assigned to a company." Marcus nods and leans in close.
"I overheard one of the instructors talking about an increase of pirates coming from the Confederation's borders. their apparently being paid a lot of money to harass shipping lanes on our side of the border." I think for a moment before I respond.
"I know the Confederation and the Independent Islands Alliance have never been on great terms but you can't really think they'd hire cutthroats to harass us." Marcus shrugs his shoulders.
"Maybe it's all just rumor but we've both seen the reports. Pirate ship takes a prize and heads over the border. If the feds weren't paying them than why aren't their border fleets stopping them?" I lean back in my chair and rub the beginnings of a beard.
"Perhaps your right. Still doesn't matter, if they send us out

there we'll kill the marauders before they get over the border." Marcus opens his mouth to say something but before he can a woman's voice interjects.

"You two done gossiping or do you want to graduate and actually find out what our first assignment is?" I look to the woman who has taken a seat on the other side of Marcus. Her short red hair and bright blue eyes have tricked many a poor man into trying to court Sam. To those brave souls who attempted they tended to get kicked to the curb, a situation I recall almost being in at one point in time at the beginning of the year.

Like Marcus and I Sam was dressed in the uniform but unlike us she was sitting with perfect posture. She was ever the proper woman even if she had a short fuze, two traits that have seen many elbows get hit by spoons. I nodded to her but before I can reply I see our head instructor walking towards the podium. As I stand up and salute him the rest of the class does the same.

When he gets to the podium I see him glance over all of us before he returns our salute. As we stand at parade rest he begins speaking in the same monotone voice that has both risen our hopes and delivered pure terror to our souls. "When you all first came through the gates behind me you were common men and woman. Now all I see is the very best Blade has to offer. Not only have several of you broken records at this center that have stood strong for decades but the very number of graduates is a new record itself. All of you have a bright future ahead of you, and now the best of you shall give a final speech before you are all sent on leave before your first assignments as members of the Combined Arms. Conner Green. Step forward and give your class's goodbye speech."

As he steps down I get up and head over to the podium. Looking down on my fellow classmates I can't help but smile. "All of you know I come from a long line of royal guards, and as such spent my childhood being trained to follow in their footsteps. I can tell you now that I have never nor will I ever find myself in more skilled company than you all. Every one of you has shown me new ways to improve myself that no royal guard could ever hope to understand." Several of them nod and I can even make out the instructor smile at the barb towards the royal guard.

"I thank you all for what you have taught me this last year. I can only hope that we may all strive to bring honor and glory to his majesty and that all of us may one day meet again to tell our tales of adventure." At that many of my fellow student applaud and I turn as the instructor comes over to me.

As he shakes my hand he hands me the red braids that signaled that I was a sgt. He then turns and waves the rest of the first row up. In short order i'm joined by Marcus, Sam, and seven others. The instructor looks at us before turning towards the rest of the students.
"As per tradition the top ten students shall be formed into their own squad. Since there are so many of you this year it has also been decided that you shall all make up the fifth company of the twenty-first regiment. You shall all find your orders in the next couple days, but for now you have all earned a celebration. I leave you now and hope to see you return one day to pass on your own experience to a new generation."

At his dismissal we all begin to head towards the gate. Some of us would head home to see families that we have only spoken to through letters, others would simply head over to the Combined Arms headquarters to get settled in. I for one look towards Marcus who nods towards Blades capital city of Ironhall.

From here we can make out the towers that sprout out from a massive stone wall that surrounds the great castile of Blade where the king seat with his family and the royal guard. The castle itself was magnificent, showing to all that visited the strength of Blade. Its high bastions showed what height we can reach, the fine stone walls of the palace let all who saw it know we have master craftsmen, and the constant flow of royal guards on the battlements and around the castile reassured the people that we have not given up our proud martial traditions like so many other islands.

Several towns and villages surround the castile to form a city that serves as Blade's capital called Hauptas. While other islands had their capitals be the home of their best merchants and tradesmen Hauptas was home to the islands military. As a given the Royal guard were based in the castile, but surprising to outsiders was that the Combined Arms and army headquarters could be found just outside the castle walls. Because of this all of the inhabitants of Hauptas were ethir members of the military or close family to those who where.

Turning away from the splendid view of the capital I look to Marcus and Sam.
"So what are you two doing for your first day off?" Sam looks to the East where a series of cottages could just barely be seen in the distance.
"I'll be heading home. I can't wait to see my siblings again."

Marcus shrugged his shoulders.
"Well i'll let you go off to get attacked by you brothers and sisters. I for one plan to head to Hafen with some of our new squadmates. You should come with is Sgt." He says Sgt sarcastically and I smile as I look to the West where the smoke clouds hide the major port city of Hafen.

Hafen was the largest port on the island and as such was the main center of trade. Because of the great of abundance of raw materials coming from merchants tradesmen set up shop there. As Blade became more active in foreign affairs Hafen grew richer and more refined. Its factories contributed over twenty percent of all arms and armor for Blades military and its massive dockyards housed the first fleet as well as naval high command. It also had some of the best inns and restaurants on Blade due to the high number of wealthy merchants and foreign dignitaries.

Shaking my head I point towards the mountains off to the North.
"I plan on heading home as well. It's been far too long since i've last seen the Greenlands."

The Greenlands were named after my ancestors who served the first king of Blade when he was just in charge a clans defenses. While the royal family eventually settled where Hauptas now stands my ancestors choose to mainly stay in the mountain territory we called home. To most it is seen as where the king's most loyal servants and friends reside the rocks reaching towards the clouds held much more.

Marcus groins but reluctantly puts his hand out. As I shake it I think back on all the training we've done together. Smiling I turn to Sam and shake hers as well. We may be separating now but soon we'll be meeting up again as the first squad of the fifth company of the twenty-first regiment.

Chapter 2
Homecoming
Conner

12/29/1438

Walking along the mountain trail I look up to see the great walls of Sicherheit. The walls were made of the same stone of the mountains that surround the villages beyond. At of the wall was a giant iron gate that stood three times my height and behind that steel double doors that made the only entrance and exit to Sicherheit. All along the wall were holes with the barrels of machine guns pointed towards the trail. Besides the royal family this was the heavestly protected place on Blade. As I get closer to the gate several of the machine guns turn towards me but stop as their operators recognize me. Before I get their the gate is opening and I see the place I of my birth.

Past the gatehouse stands hundreds of houses, several large stone barracks, as well as many large warehouses. All throughout the area children were running or fighting each other while adults watched. To the unaware this would seem normal, but these children were not playing or roughhousing. They were being trained to be some of the deadliest soldiers on earth. The adults were their instructors and as I walked by I saw one of them demonstrating how to snap a neck.

As I pass adults and children alike salute me. I return everyone of them until my arm feels like it may fall off. After another round of salutes I make it to a my destination. A small house with no windows and a unusually large chimney that belched out smoke. Knocking on the door I wait a minute before the door opens to reveal a long haired man roughly my age wearing a leather apron with tools hanging in straps of fabric. It would be hard to tell if the man's hair was black or if it was the same soit and oil that stained his apron.

When he wipes some hair out of his eyes I one blue and one green. As he looks me up and down he smiles and steps aside.
"Conner! I guess your training is done then?" I smile as I enter the workshop. As my eyes adjust I see the forge that is the source of the smoke and along all the walls blueprints were spread out. Several workbenches were laid out with tools and metal contraptions on them.

"I see that your still as engaged in your work as ever Gearbox." Gearbox's smile grows as he shuts and locks the door.
"Of course! If I don't have any projects I start to go a little stir crazy."

I look at one of the metal contraptions on the desk. At one point in my life i'd of started to mess with it but after a close call with a new explosive compound i'd learned that touching something in Gearbox's was a good way to lose some fingers. He walks over and picks it up for me to see. As far as I can tell it was a metal ball. Common sense would tell me its a toy but since its Gearbox it could be anything.

"It's a new type of grenade i've been working on. Bit of a short fuse and doesn't have the most impressive explosion, but it does unleash quite a bit of shrapnel." I stare at the ball with new found caution.

"Have you tested them yet?" He puts the ball back on the table.

"All the trials have gone well. They shred the bark of groves of trees with consistency but the army prefers the older models that just blow everything up." I look at the grenade and grimace.

"If you want I can take some with me if I get deployed. They'd probably be used against pirates and I imagine it'll work well in the confines of a ship." Gearbox pulls out a notepad and writes some numbers down.

"I'll get some ready. Don't worry about pick up ethir, i'll send them to CA HQ. You can pick them up there when you get summoned."

I nod. CA's were given a standard kit but were allowed and often encouraged to add their own gear. With a man like Gearbox in my corner that means i'll probably have a lot of custom work mixed in. As I'm thinking that he walks over and grabs a case and places it on a table.

Walking over he opens it to reveal the handle of a sword but instead of a blade there was a rectangle piece of metal. The metal wasn't that long and would probably be about half the size of a normal blade. When Gearbox takes it out I see the metal was hiding a blade inside it. Flicking a switch on the handle the blade extends and locks into place at the end of the metal and creates a full sword.

Whistling I admire the craftsmanship.

"I can see that coming in handy. Certainly be easy to hide if nothing else." Gearbox hands me the sword and I give it a couple test swings. It was well balanced but was shorter than i'd previously thought.

"I made it to compliment your swordsmanship. Not only is it

fast on the draw but you can use it in combination with your standard sword. Should be helpful when boarding ships or fighting multiple opponents."

I nod. After a couple more test swings I locate the latch and fold the blade back into place. Gearbox hands me a sheath and I strap it to my belt on my right side, opposite of where my sword was. While I insured the sword was secure Gearbox headed over to another workbench where several boxes were stacked.

"I got a couple other things in the works you'd find interesting but i'm sure you didn't come here just to get free stuff." He stops and look over to me. "At least I hope not." I tap the pommel of my new sword.
"As much as I enjoy your new toys I did come here to see how your doing old friend." He smiles.
"Good as I can ever get. Father is in Hauptas delivering a shipment of new rifles and mother is off with Tink buying some ore for us to use. Besides that the years been rather calm all things considered." I look over the walls with blueprints covering almost every inch.
"Last time I was in here you had some wall space left. How'd that new pistol work out?" Gearbox's smile turns into a frown.
"Horrible. It'll tear through a concrete wall but it requires you to be at pointblank. Add in the fact that the large caliber of the bullet makes it impossible to make the gun anything but a single shooter makes it a horrible weapon compared to others." I smile as I look all around the workshop.

"If you made it I can't imagine it'd be anything but the best. You still have it?"

Shrugging Gearbox heads over to a cabinet that was hidden in the corner and stars rummaging through it. While muttering under his breath. After a few minutes he picks something out and comes back. He hands me a box and I in turn place it on a mostly empty workbench to open it.

Inside I find a pistol with a long barrel with a wooden support under it that runs all the way back to the large camber. Picking it up I see it has a similar design to a revolver and pull the barrel down. Looking into the chamber the smirk i'd been wearing up to this point falls off. As I pull out the intergantly carved bullet I notice the pointed tip and sear size of the thing.

"Don't see bullets this size. Too big to be considered conventional and not big enough to be artillery." Gearbox nods as he hands me another box.
"Thirteen millimeter rounds with a chemical mix that makes it about as strong as a artillery shell if used right." I open the small box and see twenty bullets neatly lined up.
"You mentioned it needed to be used pointblank. Also i'm guessing it takes a bit to make these bullets." Gearbox nods and reaches over to take one of the bullets out of the pack.
"The closer you are to your target the better. It loses its bite after only about ten yards away and will either shot wide or explode in mid-air. I had wondered if I could make it a type of hand mortar but I shelved it in favor of other projects."
As he examines the bullet I walk over to a worktable with some leather straps and fashion a crude sling to attach to my back just above my butt. Putting the pistol in it I give it a few test tugs to insure its firm before turning back to gears.

"I don't suppose you could make a more permanent holster?" He walks over and exams my work a moment before shrugging.

"I'll whip something up tomorrow and send it your way. Not sure why you'd want the thing through." I shrug as I start heading towards the door.

"We should get drinks soon. Until then make sure to keep up the good work."

Heading outside I look off into the distance where a large stone barracks can be seen. Walking towards it old memerors assail me. As a child I was always the most rebellions and was one of the only kids that skipped any parts of training. I'd often hide in the old barracks until my father would come and find me. He was always the only one who could find me without any problems.

Shaking myself out of my memory I look around as I get closer and see my families name engraved in steel atop of the door. The Green family had wealth to rival the king, the complete trust and faith of the people they swore to protect. Many of Blades scholars debate how we got our status, the answer is with the blood of our ancestors.

Getting to the large double doors I push them open to reveal a wide open room. Looking up I can see a stone platform with two stairways leading to it from the ground. On the walls to either side of me is doors that lead to other rooms that've been vacant for hundreds of years. Heading up the stairs I let my hand glide across the railing just like I used to as a child.

When I get to the top i'm at another double door. Opening them up I see a hallway leading towards a open area. Walking down the hall I pass several portraits of my ancestors. Some painting are of young men and woman with smiles or smirks, but most of them are of people dressed in uniforms or plate mail. Getting to the end of the hall I start hearing the banging of steel against steel and head towards it. Exiting the hall I find several routes to other parts of the barracks but head down the hall where the noise is coming from. Getting to a open door I find the people who call this desolate place their home.

Two people dressed in full plate armor were sparing in the center of a ringed room. Watching them was my father in his royal guard armor. While the Combined Arms switched to uniforms long ago the royal guards prefer their red steel plated armor to protect their king. Over the years the design has changed as smiths discovered ways to make the armor lighter or stronger until the current designers boost that it could stop a cannon.

The two in the middle wore a similar design but instead of blood red theirs was a cold black that made them appear as shadows. Black marked them out as apprentices to the royal guard. Walking over to the royal guard observing the match I lean against the wall.

"I see those two finally got their armor. Guess you can finally stop worrying about our duty now." As I speak the clash of metal halts as the two stop to stare at me. The royal guard turns to me and I see through the slits in his helmet the anger in his eyes.

"What concern is it of yours? I figured you'd be out getting drunk with the rest of your ilk." I stare into his eyes before heading over to a rack and grabbing a dull sword.

"Figured i'd come and show my old man what i'd learned."
The royal guard grunts as he grabs one of the apprentices
swords.

"There is nothing they could of taught you that is of any
value. Unless you plan to steal my sword or poison my
wine."

Stepping into the ring I assume a defensive stance as he does
the same opposite. Time seems to come to a halt as we both
size each other up. While our two branches have always
maintained that the other was incompetent it was never a
good idea to underestimate your opponent. Seeing him shift
his stance slightly I throw myself towards him hoping to
catch him unaware.

I aim my thrust towards his neck but before my blade gets
there he deflects it with his own. Before he can counter I
jump back to distance myself. As I resume my defencive
stance he charges towards me. His blade seems to be heading
towards my shoulder but instead of countering it I side step it
and put out my leg to trip him up.

Causing him to stumble was too much to hope for but I did
manage to force him towards the wall. Gripping my sword
with two hands I begin hacking away at him, not giving him a
chance to rest while at the same time pushing him closer to
the wall. Just as his back touches the wall he uses it as
leverage to send a devastating kick to my chest.

The kick knocks all the air from my lungs and sends me back
a couple steps. Somehow I maintain my footing but now he
standing ready to deliver his own offensive. As he raises his

sword to strike me from above I drop my sword and slide under his legs. Before he can turn I jump onto his back and put him into a headlock.

With his air suddenly cut of he drops his sword to grab my arms. His grip is like steel and my arms beg for mercy but I do not let go of his neck. Slowly the straight in his grip grows weaker and as he falls to a knee I release my grip. While he regains his breath I rub my arms in an attempt to get feeling back in them.

After a minute he rises to his feet and glares in my direction. "I see they taught you something useful." I nod
"And it would seem you haven't lost your grip in your old age." He scuffs as he grabs his sword and looks towards the two apprentices.
"Let this be a reminder to you two. Always protect your neck and joints! Your armor can't help you there and a experienced voe will use that against you."

The two nod and the royal guard turns back to me. He extends his hand and I accept it.
"Welcome home son."

Chapter 3
Politics
Conner

12/29/1438

Looking around the table I smile as I see my brother and sister. Like me they had dark brown hair and bright blue eyes. They were four years younger than me but they hardly hung of my coattails the way most younger siblings do. No Lora and James had always followed their own paths and while they backed my decision to join the Combined Arms they decided that they'd be better off in the guard.

Thinking back to when they helped me ward off the rest of my family when I decided not to join the guard like tradition. If not for them I doubt i'd be allowed on these grounds or even the privilege of my last name. Turning to my father I see his grey hair and the joy in his eyes. After mom died he doubled his efforts in the guard and our training. When the rest of the family tried to oust me when I turned my back on tradition he was the only member of the royal guard to give his blessing after my siblings had talked to him.

All of us being together hasn't happened for a year. And not only that but this may be the first time a member of the royal guard and the Combined Arms have ever eaten at the same table without complaining. To this day it's hard to pinpoint when the professional rivalry turned so bitter but now even the king could not get the two to get along.

"Where do you think you'll be deployed?" This question was asked by Lora. Turning towards her I shrug my shoulders. "Not sure. Heard we might get sent pirate hunting but since we're the new fifth company of the twenty-first regiment we might just be given some covert mission to get our feet wet." Father shakes his head at this.

"His majesty won't be sending your company on any covert ops any time soon. After the defensive pact with the UIA is signed he'll have plenty of experienced agents to do any future work."

I eat some bread as I think about where I might be sent in my head. Since Blade was on the the edge of southern explored territory it was close to both the borders of the UIA and the Imperium. Because of this the Combined Arms was formed to serve as both the first responders to any conflict with these two factions but also to head intelligence. This meant that CA squads could be sent as volunteers to help other islands in the Alliance, or they could find themselves gathering information or even attempting to influence other factions to benefit Blade.

For the last couple decades the Alliance has been trying to get a defensive treaty with the UIA to make the Confederation and Imperium think twice before invading. Till just a couple weeks ago their stance had been that sighing such a treaty would simply encourage a similar deal between the other two. All that changed when the Confederation started funding pirates to operate in both our factions waters.

After that was revealed to the public the UIA agreed to sign a mutual defence treaty so long as it included the condition that both our factions increase anti-pirate efforts. The condition calls for a increase of patrol fleets as well as task forces who would actively hunt pirates and attempt to find their hideouts.

James shook his head.
"I don't see why the king doesn't just send the CA across the border to find whoever pays the bastards. I'm sure if the extra incentive to attack us was there than the feds will have a pirate problem just like us." Father pours himself a glass of wine before responding.
"If those involved were all just low-lifes than your plan would work. But if rumors ring true than many of these so called pirates are 'former' members of the Confederation's navy. So the CA would be looking for men in uniform rather than fat merchants." I nod as I sip from my own glass.
"People may complain if a merchant winds up dead or a government official is found to be in another factions pocket. People will call for war if soldiers start dropping dead."
James rubs his head at our words while Lora perks up.
"So any CAs in the Confederation will probably be looking where these 'former' navy men are hanging around. That way the patrols can know where to expect them." James face grows pale as he turns to me.
"If you do hunt pirates do you think you might go after Bloody Jack?" I raise my eyebrows.
"Who?"
Father puts his glass aside as he turns to glare at James before turning to me.
"Bloody Jack is a butcher. While other pirates hunt merchant ships she goes after bigger prizes. She's only been active for a year now and she's sunk or captured two patrols on top of raiding several islands on the border. Lots of blood on her hand and she doesn't seem interested in retirement."

I look at James and Lora. They both seem more man slightly

wary of this Jack. Considering they had me as an older brother that's saying something. Setting my plate aside I look to Lora.

"Enough talk of pirates. Tell me about being in the guard?" Lora's eyes beam and James seems to relax a little.

"Its great. We get to learn a lot from the others and even though we're just shadows at the moment we kinda like our jobs." James shifts some of the food on his plate around.

"I think you like the whole shadow thing more than me. I personally can't wait to stand tall while I guard his majesty."

Glancing at my father I give him a knowing smile. He and I both knew that James was a lot like me when it came to our wonderlust. If not for his connection to his twin he'd probably have joined me in the Combined Arms. Probably for the best since they complement each other so well.

James likes to fix problems as simply as possible and has a problem with thinking outside the box. His strengths lie more in the area of combat and his remarkable perception. On the other hand Lora finds upfront combat old fashioned and prefers fighting as far away as possible. She also thinks the best way to deal with a problem is to stop it before it becomes one.

If the royal guard was just tall red armored guards like my father Lora probably would find herself lacking. Thankfully for her the guard is really two groups. The first group is the royal guard themselves, the big red armor wards off common assassins and their training helps them deal with any serious attacks on the royal family. As far as the public is concerned that's all there is to it, but the guard have shadows.

Shadows are aptly named as they work behind the scenes to

inspect and investigate any potential threats to the royal family. Where their red brothers stay close to the king in the capital shadows operate all over the island. Typically they just keep tabs on foreigners but if they think someone is a possible danger to the throne they'll take action.

"You should get some rest. I can get a car to take you to base in the morning." I nod my appreciation.
"Thank you father. As much i'd like to stay a couple days longer I would hate to be the last of my squad to report in."

Setting my plate to the side I get up from my chair and prepare to head to bed. Before I go I look back to my father and siblings all sitting at one table. I understand why Sam would miss her family so.

On my way to my room I see a new painting on the wall. It was me after I first got my uniform last month. Looking at it I see the dark green suit and hat with the interlocked sword and pistol. In the portrait I looked rather bored if not sad due. I've never had a problem sitting still but standing still while smiling like an idiot had always been a problem.

Looking at the portrait I remember all the hard work it took to earn it. Not only that but I felt a surge of pride as it sunk in that it was the only portrait of its kind. There were countless paintings of my ancestors on these walls but not a single one wore the uniform of the Combined Arms. Smiling I stare at the portrait for a moment. I wonder what stories will come to the minds of my descendants when they see this. Perhaps they'll be inspired to break tradition too and do something besides serve in the guard.

Chapter 4
Briefing
Conner

1/05/1438

Seating at a table I look across at captain Steel. His face bore the scars of battle and his brown hair was well past regulation length. His dark blue eyes gave me a once over and after a moment he passes me a folder.

"In there is your first orders. Your squad will be aboard one of the first ships to take the fight to the doorsteps of the pirates." I pick up the folder and open it. As I read through the papers the captain continues. "With the deal with the UIA we can take the ships we had guarding our border with them and put them to better use. Our part of the defence fleet has just returned and is already being refitted to head up North to our border with the feds."

I stop my reading as I look at the photo of a ship. At first glance she was a typical destroyer. Two smoke stacks for the engines and several cannons lining the hull. What caught my eye was the lack of long range armements. Sure a destroyer wouldn't have many long range guns since they primarily served as escorts but most have at least two or three on their top deck. This one just had anti-air guns at the bow and stern.

"I see you've taken an interest in the ship you'll be serving on." I look up to see the captain smirking. Nodding my head

I put the photo on the deck.

"I don't recall this design during my studies sir." He shakes his head.

"Figures. They really should update quicker if they don't want some newbies looking like fools. Anyway this is a new type of destroyer Blades been toying with. Heavy armor with an abundance of close range weapons that'd make most people think its outdated. The idea came from a pirate that's been using a similar design to take down ships at a record pace." I stare at the picture. Lack of long range guns, heavy armor, and inspired by a pirate...

"So it's a ship designed for boarding actions." Steel looks pleased.

"Your quick on the uptake. The pirate in question uses it to board patrol ships on the border. Since no one's interested in getting a court martial the rest of the patrol joins in to help their comrades only to find themselves outmatched by a bunch of pirates. The end result is a patrol of ships that can be sold for tens of thousands of Confederate pounds."

I nod. A ship's crew tends to be trained to prevent boarding attempts and even the smallest military vessel has a squad of marines in case someone does get aboard. But if a ship with a crew dedicated to boarding sunk their hooks into a ship the marines would likely be overwhelmed or outgunned. Leaning back I start asking the questions on my mind.

"How many crew does a ship like this have?"

"Ours has three hundred sailors and five hundred marines plus a squad of CAs."

"What's the ships armament?"

"Twelve breech-loading cannons on port and starboard. Two flak guns on the bow and stern."

"Are we to be an attachment or under the ship's captain?"

"You'll find that CAs always serve as attachments. If you think that captain is needlessly risking the lives of your squad feel free to ignore him. Just don't go ignoring any plans he sets up and costing him any livers ethier and everything should be fine."

"How long is deployment?"

"The ships will be stationed at the island of Waters and return to Blade every three months for a one month leave. Your squad is to stay at Water until the pirate problem has died down."

"Is Water's shipping being singled out?"

"No but several islands on the border have been raided by a pirate called bloody Jack including Water. Death tolls in the thousands and the boarder islands are pressing the council hard for more support."

I stop for a moment to think. The council was made up of representatives from each of the twenty-seven islands that make up the Alliance. Their job is to serve as a representatives to other islands and maintain a combined army and navy to defend us. They have also made laws that are universal across all twenty-seven islands but that hardly ever happens and the only time that comes to mind is when slavery was made a crime some three hundred odd years ago.

Including Water there are seven islands near the northern border. All of these islands rely heavily on trade and in return for money and goods they get military protection from the council or individual islands. The islands there are a large part of the Alliance's economy, their only rival is the islands bordering the UIA and since they came up with this treaty it must be assumed their trade is being affected as well.

If the council as a whole sees this a problem it's not just an ambitious pirate. To get the council and the UIA to see it as a problem it must be like a war out there. Or at the very least the amount of shipping lost is starting to be felt by those in charge. Times like this i'm glad Blade only really needs our neighbors Verbun and Alleato. Both are within a couple days travel and through them Blade gets rare metals and other raw materials to equip our armies as well as food to feed our people.

"If you have no further questions you should brief your men. The Wolfhunter is being christened by the king tomorrow so you need to be ready." I give the captain a quizzical look.
"Wolfhunter sir?" He taps the photo.
"The ship you'll be serving on until this pirate problem is dealt with." I nod.

Getting up from my chair I pick up the folder and head out. Passing through the rest of the base I finally make it back to the entrance to find Markus and Sam waiting in the lobby. As I approach they both salute me.
"At ease." I hold up the folder "I got our first mission. Looks like we're gonna be hunting pirates!"

With that both of them break into smiles. We were concerned that our company would never see any action yet here we getting the best chance at action a man can hope for. We truly are some lucky bastards.

Chapter 5
Christening
Jade

1/06/1438

Looking in the mirror I was as the servants put the finishtouchs on my dress. Wiping away a strand of my blond hair I wonder how much trouble i'd get in for cutting it. As i'm pondering this one of the maids tugs on a cord and I feel my waist constrict as the dress does it's best to kill me. The long puffy thing was extremely tight and required two people just to get the damn thing on. The head maid Claire takes a step back and admires her work.

"Your beautiful your highness."

I focus on my face in the mirror. Under all the makeup that I can only imagine is supposed to make it look like i'm blushing constantly i'd say I look good. All the makeup is a pain in of itself but what's killing me is the dress. It's just so tight!

"If this dress kills me I want it hanged."

As Claire frowns at my words I hear an all too familiar grunt. Turning to see my father's personal guard I see he's in his red plate armor as always. He doesn't say anything, he doesn't need to.
"Well Claire it seems it's time for me to go. Make sure to actually take a break while i'm gone ok?"

Claire returns to her normal smile as she glared daggers at the guard. She's worked here going on forty years but still hasn't gotten used to the royal guards. Can't say I blame her since all they seem to do is stand around staring at people until someone gives them an order.

"I'll make sure to rest my feet your highness. I'll see you upon your return as always." As I leave she and the other maids bow.

Following the guard through the long hallways of the castile we pass several guards and every now and again a servant. I remember reading books that talked about so many people being in the castile from all over it felt like a market. Now you only see people wondering the halls if they work here.

Eventually we get to the main entrance where four more red guards join us as we leave. I've no doubt there's at least twice as many of those shadow ones keeping an eye on me as well. Approaching a very luxurious car one of the guards opens the door and heads in first. After a second a red gauntlet appears and I grab it.

As I take my seat I see my father across from me. My father looked just like the kings I remember reading about when I was a little girl. Long golden hair, and bright blue eyes, if someone had told me he came out of a painting i'd agree.

"Thank you for fetching her Daniel." The guard who'd been escorting me nods but says nothing. They rarely do unless father is asking for their opinion. "Do you remember what to do Jade?" I roll my eyes. How stupid does he think I am?
"All I have to do is go up there and smash a bottle against a

boat and yell Wolfhunter. Not that difficult." My father stares at me a moment as if to say 'I don't trust you!'

"Just remember not to add anything to the script ok." I shrug.

"I don't know what you expect me to 'add'." He rubs his temple.

"Remember the time you met with that onvoy? I do, he does, and so does his island." I think back for a moment but can't seem to remember doing anything wrong.

"All I remember is asking how he enjoyed the lake." My father nods.

"And then after he presented you a necklace from prince Bellarine you threw him in the lake." I smile as I think back to the stunned look on my father's face. I thought he might pop a vein when he was yelling at me later.

"What was the problem? You told me I needed to decline didn't you?"

For a moment I think he might start yelling but Danial grunts. When my father looks his way he calms down and takes a breath. For several minutes we don't say anything.

"Daniel I hear your son is a part of the crew for this ship. Is that correct?" I glance over to Daniel. I'd always heard of the oh so loyal family Green who I could always count on to help.

"I thought all Greens were in the guard?" He shifts his head to look towards his king for a moment before turning back to the window. Father looks over to me.

"He decided to serve me in the Combined Arms. He's actually leading a squad on board the Wolfhunter."

I glance over to Daniel. Every Green i've ever met were in the guard and every time I heard about one was when they joined or left the guard. This may be the first time in Blades history one of them broke that tradition.

Here I thought I was the only one on this island that broke tradition. Wonder if he was as silent as his father or if he couldn't shut up? Oh maybe he's the dashing rogue type? Really so long as he's not just another knight in shining armor i'd enjoy talking to him.

"I must confess father, i'm interested in this rouge Green. Don't suppose he's one of the people i'm supposed to shake hands with?" My father looks at me a moment before answering.
"If you recall I told you you'd be shaking hands with the captain, the ranking marine, and the ranking CA. So yes you'll be shaking his hand. Why are you interested?" My father looks at me with more than a hint of worry in his eyes.
"What? A Green not a part of the guard is like a bird without feathers. Anyone would be interested."

He glances at Daniel. Not getting a response my father opens his mouth when a knock from the divers divider grabs our attention.

"I guess were here. Jade for our ancestors sake don't do anything i'll regret."

Stepping out of the car I see a huge crowd of people cheering. There was a wide passage through the crowd with several red guards staring at the people. As my father and I made our way down the street Daniel and the other guards form around us and we both wave to our people. Some children are throwing flowers our way and I turn and smile to them.

When we get closer I see the new destroyer's bow waiting to be dropped into the sea. I'm not the biggest fan of boats but even I must admit that seeing such a well made vessel ready to set sail is a sight to behold. In front of the vessel was a podium overseeing the hundreds of crewmen that'll be calling this ship home soon.

Getting up to the podium father takes the stand and addresses the crowd.

"It is with great pride I stand before you all today. To see the first of ten ships that'll be taking back the seas from those who would use it as their own playground. The men and women of this fine vessel will be the first Blade sends to stop the pirate menace on the border. All of you should feel honor for the task you have been chosen but know that your job is far more than hunting pirates. Your deeds on the border will remind our fellow islands that Blade stands ready! Remind them that while we may be far from their precious trade routes we stand ready to aid our allies when they are in need."

As father stops talking the crowd erupted into applause. Even the sailors and marines can be seen slapping each others back and smiling as they release the honor their job brings to them and Blade as a whole. I must admit i'm rather jealous. Thye get to leave for adventure while I must stay here and learn the ways of court and diplomacy.

A nodge on my shoulder reminds me that it's my turn to please the crowd. Getting up from my seat I head over to where a bottle has been suspended by a rope. Grabbing it in my hands I look out to the crowd.

"This vessel shall forever more be known as the Wolfhunter. May it's history be both long and honorable, and may our enemies learn to fear its might!" As the last words leave my lips I toss the bottle and shatters on the steel hull of the ship.

Stepping back I ignore the cheers of the crowd that have become almost wild. Instead I focused on my father as he nods towards me. Heading to his side I follow as he heads towards the front row of the crew where three men rose to salute us. The first man looked to be in his forties and wore a long raincoat and a trifold hat that hid most of his features. As my father shook his hand and wished him luck on his voyage I was able to make out the dark green eyes filled with pride as well as the stubble covering his chin.

Shaking his hand I thank him for his service and proceed down the line. The second man who my father was finishing with was dressed in the dark blues of the marines and also seemed to be in his forties. His short brown hair matched his eyes and his face was clean shaven. Shaking his hand I can feel him holding back, perhaps he worried he'd crush my delicate hand in his own.

Passing him I wish him a safe voyage and arrive at the person i'd be thinking about for the last half hour. Taking a moment to look at him it was odd to think he came from the same stock as the man behind the read armor of my fathers personal guard. Admittedly I have never seen his father's face I can't imagine him ever sporting a grin that practically drooled excitement at the adventure ahead. If his boyish grin didn't betray his excitement than his blue eyes practically sparkle, but not at the prospect of shaking hands with his future queen.

No his eyes may seemed to be looking at me but I can tell the only thing he sees is the ship behind me. Holding out my hand I am surprised that he takes a second before grasping it with a iron grip. Looking him in his bright blue eyes I watch as his grin turns into a smile and he relaxes his grip.

"Sorry ma'am. Must be all the excitement." I return his smile and increase the pressure of the handshake.
"No problem. You'll find i'm not as delicate as I look." I see out of the corner of my eyes the others glancing my way expecting me to move on.

Releasing his hand I continue smiling at him and begin walking away. Getting close to father I lean close to whisper to him.

"I'll be keeping my eye on this Green." My father cast a glance towards him and I do likewise.
"He's an odd one when compared to his family that's for sure. I myself am also interested in where his path will lead."

Chapter 6
Waters
Conner

1/13/1438

Looking at the bustling port I stop counting the ships coming and going. There are far too many ships here for any navy to hope to protect. Even with the ten wolf ships here the merchant ships outnumber military ships at least ten times over. I'm glad i'm not in charge of protecting those merchants, no way they can ever hope to guard all of them once they set sail.

"GREEN! The captain wishes to speak to you." I nod toward the sailor.

Heading away from the view I open one of the hatches on the deck. Heading down I pass several sailors going about their duties and a couple squads of marines practicing. Navigating the narrow corridors I eventually make it to the captain's quarters. Knocking on the door I wait until I hear an invitation.

After a minute the door opens and the ranking marine, first Lieutenant Holland was in full dress and welcomed me in. Entering the room I see even the captain's room was a little cramped, just big enough to fit a fold out bed and a desk. Sitting behind the desk was captain Logang. Standing at attention I wait until he speaks.

"You ever been to Water sgt?" I shake my head.
"No sir. First time i've left the island sir." He nods as he

grabs a map and unrolls it on the desk.

"Then take a look. As you can see the island is above normal in size with several cities. The reason for this is because of the rivers linking the cities to the sea, allowing all of them to act as trade nodes throughout the island. This not only allows for more traffic to come through but also makes defending the island rather simple." I nod as I take in the map.

For the most part the island was flat with only a couple major forests to offset the number of cities spread all over the map. There were several large rivers all throughout the island and even more small rivers and lakes. It would appear the island was mostly water from the map.

"With every city having a trade port it's not hard to see how Water became one of the richest islands in the Alliance." Captain Logang tapped a city with several major rivers connecting it to half the other cities as well as three different routes to open water.

"We'll be stationed at the capital Wessar. Today we're going to drop in and have the king inspect the Wolfhunter. It shouldn't take more than a couple hours and in that time we'll be restocking on supplies for our first hunt." Holland walks up to the desk and rolls up the map.

"We aren't ones for fancy dinners or balls. With any luck we'll be in and out before the sun sets." I nod.

"I can respect that sir. I'll make sure my squad knows not to wonder."

Saluting them I exit the room. Heading to were the squad was birthed I find several of them playing cards while Markus and Sam cleaned their swords. As I enter all of them stand at attention and I wave them down.

"We'll be making a pitstop at Waters before we begin our hunt. Don't stray from the ship or the rest of us will be forced to gain fame and glory without you." They all call out their affirmatives and I head over to Sam and Markus.

"Sam I need you to make sure our post here is set up. It should be near the dock, go there and let me know what it has and what it needs." Sam nods and goes over to the rest of the gang. When she's gone I look at Markus and smile. "How long until we get to prove our mettle?" Markus taps the hilt of his sword.

"Not long sarge. If rumors sing true than the border is being overwhelmed by pirates." I shrug.

"If only. I find it hard to believe pirates can ever be more than a minor nuisance to any island." Markus shakes his head.

"If there wasn't some merit to the rumors the UIA wouldn't have signed a treaty over them. Speaking of the UIA you think we'll be heading that way after we leave port?" I head over to my bunk.

"I don't think we'll be in UIA water's any time soon. We have to clear our own front yard before we can help our neighbors." He nods as he sits opposite me.

"I hope we get to the cleaning part soon. I didn't spend a year just to wait on a boat while another king inspects us." Taking out some reports I begin reading them.

"Markus if you want you can read reports with me until we find something to fight." He leans over and grabs a couple files.

"Guess I might as well, but I had planned on seeing what kind of food Waters has to offer." I laugh.

"Food? I'll bet you were after something more liquid." Markus flips through one of the folders.

"I may enjoy a good drink but I love a good meal." I smile as

I read through the reports.

Hours go by while I read. At some point the rest of the squad head out to step foot on land but Markus and I continue reading reports. It may not be the most exciting but it needs to be done. After a while the door opens and Sam enters. She heads over and passes me a new folder which I open immediately.

Reading it I nod at her report. The king of Water's has seen fit to grant us a warehouse to use as our barracks while we're here. It's on the small side and is still mostly filled with goods but Sam apparently found a way to 'deal' with the unwanted cargo. The rest of the report is just a list of things needed to turn it into a real outpost.

Grabbing a pen I sign my name on it and pass it back to Sam. She nods and sits on her own bunk to start filling out request forms. When it comes to paperwork Sam is one of the best. Even back in the first weeks of training she had a knack for logistics. Having her on the team more less guarantees i'll never be found wanting for ammo or food.

"We might have a problem with Water's nobles." I look over to Sam. "Some guards from some lord wanted to let us know how to pay taxes." I pick up another report and begin reading.
"I assume you told them where to send the bill?" Markus lets out a laugh.
"You'd think they'd leave us alone. They do know their king is inspecting our ship right?" Sam finishes a paper and glances over to me.
"I'm not joking Conner. I asked around and it seems like the local nobles would rather we left." I smile.

"Let me guess. They think it'd be better to pay the pirates to not attack them." Markus groans as Sam nods her head.

"Guess I should of figured an island who values money as much as Water would try to save money at every corner." I put the reports to the side.

"Just remember that if islands like Water didn't bring in that money Blade wouldn't be able to devote itself to the art of war. Hell even with islands like Water we still try and make as much money as we can without compromising the military." Markus grunts.

"Yeah but Blade would never even consider paying tribute to anyone. And the only time you'd find us talking to pirates is during interrogations." Sam puts away her paperwork and lays down.

"We should rest. We might find ourselves 'talking' with these pirates soon enough." We all agree and I quickly nod off.

Chapter 7
First Blood
Conner

1/13/1438

Standing just under the hatch I glance behind me at my
squad.
"Last check."

While they looked over their kits I took stock of my own. I
had my sword on my left hip and a standard six-shooter on
my right. Gearbox's pistol is in a holster on my lower back
while its bullets were on my forearms. Tapping my chest I
feel the grenades there; two of Gear's shrapnels and two
smoke. Everything set I turn to my squad.
"Alpha one is green." Markus is right behind me and gives
me a smile.
"Alpha two is green." Sam nodded behind Markus.
"Alpha three is green."

One after another all ten of us signaled green. For the rest of
the mission we will go by these numbers. No other CA
squads are here so the Alpha may be unnecessary but regs are
regs and it shouldn't hurt anything.

As i'm thinking several loud booms shake the ship and I grab
one of the railings leading up the hatch. Ignoring the fact our
ship just took fire I turn to Marcus.
"We head straight for the lower decks. Leave the top deck to
the marines." He nods.
"Understood Alpha one" As another set of explosions go off
in the distance I wonder how much damage is being done.

Before I can allow that thought to wonder a loud whistle is hear all throughout the Wolfhunter.

Taking out my sword I don't extend it yet but head up the hatch as a loud crash is heard from the bow. As the whole ship rocks I barely maintain my balance but manage to continue climbing up to the hatch. Opening the hatch i'm momentarily blinded by the light.

As my vision comes back I see the deck of the Wolfhunter. Several holes were spread throughout and as I watch other hatches fly open and men in the marines blue come out. Not wanting to be left behind I run up and head towards the bow.

Getting closer I see the other ship. A modified merchant, it had armor plates on its sides as well as several cannons and even a double barrel cannon that was probably the cause of the explosions from earlier. Its flag was a dark spot against the clear skies, its white skull signaling its owners as enemies of all.

Running across the deck i'm joined by several marines and together we reach the bow where others have already started jumping across. Not wasting time I put a foot on the railing and use it to propel me forward. While in the air I take in the situation below me.

The pirate ship was lower than ours and allowed me to take in the marines who were fighting with men in woman in all manner of clothes and armor. It doesn't take long to spot my objective. A door in the side of the ship guarded by two pirates who were firing rifles into the marines.

Hitting the deck at a run I make a beeline towards them and

before as they see me coming two shots ring out. As they fall I reach the door and open it to come face to face with young man with a pistol in his hand. Unfolding my sword with a flick I impale the man as I charge into the bowels of the ship.

Charging down the stairs I run into two others before I slam the body into a wall. Before I can take my sword out of the man i'd killed two and three step to either side of me and open fire with their pistols. As they do I make two quick stabs into the bodies of the men who i'd collided with on the stairs.

Looking around I see a stairwell leading down and the hall i'm in currently. A couple bodies were spread throughout the hall as the others had cleared the area. Signaling to two I order him to take five through eight to the left while nine and ten secure this entry. I signal for the rest to follow me and I begin sprinting down the hall.

Seeing some doors on either side of the hall I order three and four to breach the ones to the left side of the hall while I take the right. While five holds the handle I take out my pistol. Nodding to him to open it I see empty bunks and a few lockers. Going in I look around and after i'm satisfied no one is in here I head to the next door in line.

After three doors i'm about to breech another when I hear boots coming towards us from the corner. Taking a knee I look towards where the hall takes a turn and see three men and a woman running our way. Seeing as their not marines or CAs I open fire and hit the woman in neck and shoulder. The rest of my shots hit the man beside her in his chest and arm. As they go down the other two taake aim with rifles and fire.

A bullet hits the wall next to me and another slams into my left shoulder. Falling back I feel my back hit the steel floor as the others make short work of the two pirates. Five helps me up and I move my shoulder experimentally. It doesn't appear to have hit the bone or any arteries but that didn't make it hurt any less.

While three and four kept watch five bandaged up my shoulder. When he was done I reloaded my pistol and lead the squad down the hall towards where the pirates had come. As we reach the end of the hall I hear the clang of steel from above and the familiar bangs and pops of gunfire.

Peeking around the corner I see a sword being thrust my way. Dodging back I grab the hilt and pull the man into the hall. As I prepare to see him shot by my squad I see that it was two and smile a bit as he looks at us.
"Your lucky i'm fast two or you'd be in charge right now."
Two looks at us and grins.
"I'd say i'm more lucky my squadmates didn't shoot me." I nod as I step out of the hall.

Looking around I can see it's another stair well. Throwing a smoke grenade I watch as it bounces off the wall and down to the next deck. I wait until I start to see smoke and hear a couple people coughing. Nodding towards two I head down with my sword and pistol drawn.

I can just make out several figures in the smoke and slash at them with my sword. Not waiting I keep going until I get out of the smoke and take a knee. I see a man with a rifle in a doorway and fire at him. I don't land a hit but he takes cover in his room. While I provide cover I see two and three breach a door.

Unlike the upper deck they don't take chances here and two tosses in one of Gears shrapnel grenades. I hear a loud boom and then several cries of pain. I ignore it and focus on the door the man had hidden in. Taking out a shrapnel grenade I pull the pin as I walk up. Before I get there a hatch opens up in the middle and without thinking I toss the grenade in there.

I hear someone say something than a the grenade goes off. Several bits of mettle and blood escape the hatch. Not wanting another interruption I run over to the hatch and slam it shut. As I do I see four and six heading toward the door the man had hidden in. While I secure the hatch Isurvey the area and see that my squad had secured the hall and where moving down towards the other end where another stairwell was probably waiting. Seeing seven and eight coming up I signal for them to keep the stairwell we came from secure.

They nod and head over to the stairwell to make sure noone came to shoot us in the back. As I walk towards the end I see the insides of one of the rooms. I see several men and woman bleeding out of a hundred wounds. For a moment I pause at the carnage these grenades cause. Shaking my head I continue on my way, i've got no time to pity scum.

Arriving at the next stairwell I see nine and ten coming down with a squad of marines. Nodding towards their sgt I inform them our hall was and the other needed checked. He nods and orders his squad down that way. As he heads to clear the rest of this deck I head towards the stairwell and pull out a smoke.

Before I can throw it a man comes up from the stairwell and bullrushes me. He takes several shots as he slams into my gut. I gasp as all the air leaves my lungs and before I can recover more pirates charge from below. As my squad opens fire I see that the man on top of me is alive despite being shot several times. Using the smoke grenade as a improvised weapon I smash it into his skull several times until his grip on me loosens.

After he finally release me I get up and put my smoke away. As I do another man comes out from below and prepares to run me through with a kitchen knife. Before he can reach me I pull out Gear's pistol and fire. The noise is deafening in the confined halls of the ship and my ears ring from the sound.

Time seems to slow as the man is hit with the bullet. It enters his chest and his eyes grow large in shock before a shower of gore can be seen from behind him. His bodie flys back down the stairs and hits his comrades who are screaming in terror as their covered in their friends blood.

Even I am shocked by the sheer destruction this gun caused to a human body. For just an instant I see him not as a pirate but as another man and disgust rises in my mind. Before I throw up my mind recalls all the stories of murder and chaos pirates cause and the disgust dissipates. It's still there but I no longer think i'll lose my lunch.

Unofourantly for the dead man's friends they don't seem to take his gruesome death as well as I do. The few remaining pirates in the stairwell drop their weapons and stare at me in horror. Two looks to me and I nod. He proceeds to grab some rope and ties up their hands and feet.

While he does that I head down and see several stunned men and woman. I look over at them and watch as they drop their weapons and raise their hands. Three and four help two tie their hands and look around. This far down there aren't many rooms but their bigger and will require time to clear.

As i'm thinking this more marines come down. They look around at the gore and the terrified pirates then at me and my squad. I look at the others and see they all sport a wound or two but nothing major, then I look at the tied up pirates and the growing number of marines.

Looking to two I point the stairwell.
"We're done here. Let's regroup and let the marines handle the rest." Two looks surprised as do the others.
"Sir shouldn't we continue the offensive." I wave my hands to indicate the surrendered pirates.
"This isn't an offensive anymore. Let the marines handle the rest." Two looks disgruntled but nods.

Slowly he and the others head back up and I look at the man i'd shot with Gears hand cannon. Passing him by I look at my squad. They may be upset now that they won't be clearing the rest of the ship but after blood cools they'll remember that the marines are better suited to clearing the wide open rooms farther below. Through i'd be lying if I said I wouldn't want to continue the fight.

Chapter 8
Commendations
Jade

4/03/1438

Looking over the table I watch as my father smiles. He's been reading the reports from the ships he sent to help stop the pirates increasing activity on the border. If his smile was anything to go one than they've done a rather good job.

"I don't suppose you'd enlighten me on what brings you such joy father." He looks up from his report and his smile gets even wider. Nothing makes him happier than talking about his soldiers accomplishments.

"The squadron we deployed to the North has seen great success. Already they've captured twentie-four ships and over ten-thousand prisoners. On top of that they've sunk another thirty-five ships." I smile as well. Those were great results, especially since it was only their first deployment their.

"We should have a feast waiting for them. They've certainly earned it." My father nods then holds up another report.

"And a place of honor for the Wolfhunter. They've captured the most ships with a grand total of ten and taken the least casualties." I tilt my head.

"If my memory is correct then that's the ship Daniel's son is serving on." Father's smile seems like its about to split his face.

"You remember correctly. Both captain Logang and first lieutenant Holland have sent commendations for his actions and that of his squad. They've apparently caused so much terror that people are starting to call them 'Piratenjagers' or pirate hunters." I laugh.

"An apt name to be sure. What commendations is the squad up for?" My father take a report and reads it off.

"One commendation for valor under fire for the squad, one commendation for heroism for the squad, twelve red badges, and three crimson daggers."

I gasp at the mention of the crimson dagger. It was a medal awarded to those who've killed over a hundred enemy combatants with a blade. In its history only forty-seven have been granted and are second only to the medal of blade. That medal has only been granted two times in our history and was the highest honor a single soldier can achieve.

"A huge honor for their squad and regiment. Are you going to grant them these commendations?" Father glances at the small pile of reports.

"Well reports are good and all but I can't just rely on paper when it comes to this. No i'll need to talk to these men and women to make sure they earned it." He grins. "Then again Blade isn't known for exaggerating our deeds." I smile at him.

"No father we are not. I must say it's going to be pleasant to hear new exploits of our military. I'm sure Daniel is also looking forward to hearing about his son's adventures." Father's smile drops.

"Unfortunately he won't be hearing those tales from Conner's mouth. He and the rest of the Combined Arms are stationed at Water." I raise my eyebrows in surprise.

"That's news to me. I thought everyone was coming home for a month of leave." Father shifts some of the papers.

"Captain Steel wants a force there in case this bloody Jack raids. Figured it'd make more sense for a hundred CAs to stay behind than a larger detachment." I shake my head.

"I'd think giving them a break at home would be better. I'm

sure Water can take care of itself, after all the work our people did they deserve a break." Father shrugs.

"Not much to be done. I'll make sure they get home next time but for now they'll have to settle for the beaches at Water. I hear their quite nice this time of year." I shake my head.

"What's done is done I guess."

I look over to the red knight I know is Daniel. I wonder how he feels about his son not coming home anytime soon. I'm sure he'd respond with a grunt or perhaps nothing at all but even he must feel a little miffed about this. Perhaps I can talk father into letting him have some time off when he gets back. I'm sure he'd enjoy seeing his favorite bodyguard relax as much as I would.

Chapter 9
Bloody Water
Conner

4/13/1438

I woke up to the sounds of alarms. Getting out of bed I put on my uniform and grab my gear. When I finish I look around as the others rush to put on their equipment. As we all get into our squads captain Steel comes in.

"Several ports are on fire. Squads one and two will stay here to protect the capital while the rest of us investigate." Coming over to me he hands me a flare gun. "Lunch that if your under attack and we'll come running." I nod and salute him.

As the other squads get ready to move out I seek out squad two's sgt. Finding her I remember her name is Ash.

"Ash you good to be Bravo?" She nods and I giver her her instructions. "Alpha will secure the docks while Bravo fortifies the palance." She nods and goes about gathering supplies.

Signaling my squad I head out of the warehouse. It's a long walk to the port and takes a couple minutes to march there. Once we arrive I see several guards of various houses securing the ships at dock. The nobles men are quick when it comes to their lords purses. Looking out to the river I see a merchant ship coming in to dock. The ship seemed strange for some reason.

I could see the crews of the other merchants looking around them in panic. Many of them were staring at the rising smoke clouds in the distance, but the merchant coming in was different. The crew on deck was calm and showed no concern for the fires in the distance. Some of them even seemed to be smiling.

"SEAL THE PORT!" Running as fast as I could I see a couple guards look at the merchant and realize what's about to happen. Several guards shout for the chains to raise but just as the port chains start to rise the ship sails into port.

As it turns I do as well. I scream for everyone to find cover and seconds later my world gets rocked. Several cannons go off and as they explode across the port one crashes nearby and it's explosion sends me to the ground. I look around in shock as most of the guards lay in bloody chunks.

Looking towards the ship I see hundreds of pirates jumping off and slaughtering the other ships crews. Watching on the top deck was a woman with long white hair and blood red eyes. Her body masked by a crimson coat that gave off the presence of death. Looking at her I feel hatred grow in me. She was not a woman, she was a monster.

Getting up I look fall back with my squad. Once we're out of cannon range I raise my hand in the air and fire the flare. A bright white light sparks against the night sky and I wonder if the captain even made it out of the city before we came under attack.

Looking at my squad I shake my head.
"We need to get to the palace. They've got far too many for us to fight alone." The others nod solemnly and we start

running.

After a couple minutes I see the palace. Its large marble columns gave way to a wide staircase that lead to the front door. I could see the front door was shut and several guards dressed in the kings colors were setting up sandbags and boxes to make a barricade. A few members of Bravo squad could be seen around but I guess most of them were inside.

As I approach several guards raise their rifles but lower them when they see that we're friends. Heading past the half constructed barricades I get to the door when I see a rack of rifles and some crates of ammo. Stopping I pick up a rifle and fill my pockets with ammo. The others do likewise and then we enter the palace.

Getting inside I could see several people huddled around the forum while a old man looked over them. Beside him was Ash and a young woman with short brown hair. She had a rifle out and even though she was in a nightgown it was clear she was ready to fight. The old man addressed the crowd.

"Calm people! Calm! My guards shall protect these halls until the other houses can muster their forces. Until then we have the aid of the Piratenjagers." Several of the people here were families cradling children. It was clear that these were the dock workers and other tradesmen who worked in the capitol. Well the ones who haven't run away or died anyway.

Heading up to Ash a couple guards attempt to stop me but I shove my way past them. As a couple people shout out Ash and the old man look my way. While Ash smile I see the other woman pointing her rifle at me. She lowers it as she recognizes my uniform but I have to admire her instincts.

Approaching Ash the old man makes to shake my hand but I brush him off.

"Bravo one we got hostiles coming from the port. At least a couple hundred strong and very bloodthirsty. How's the defences?" Ash grimances.
"We'd be better at the warehouse. Several side entrances have only a couple of guards but I gave them what few machine guns we have. Of course this means our center is weak. We might hold the doors for a bit but once they get in this place will be a kill box." I look at the old man.
"Can you get these people out of harm's way?" The old man scratches his chin a moment.
"If they spread out they might be able to hide but besides this the only room big enough to hid them is the ballroom." I nod and look to the Ash.
"Take them there and put a couple guards with them. This the king?" I point at the old man. He smiles and makes to shake my hand again but I wave him off. As Ash nods I look towards to woman carrying a rifle. "And you?" She glares my way.
"I'm princess Samantha Waters. You should show some respect to my father." I look at the old man and he smiles again.
"I'll do all the formal shit after we're save, if we don't die of course." She looks like she's about to say something but then nods.
"Agreed. I suppose we should get to the front to wait." I glare at her.
"We?" She smiles.
"You don't think i'd cower in a corner while my people are being attacked? No a true leader will fight for their people." I look at the old man. His smile wanes but he nods his head. Looking at the night gown I put my rifle down and take off

my jacket. Passing it to her she makes to refuse it.

"You want to fight princess that's not my concern, but i'll be damned if you fight in some gown. This jacket has some armor in it and it should help you. If nothing else it makes you less of a target." She reluctantly takes the jacket and puts it on. She'll still stand out but not nearly as much as she did.

Picking up my rifle I head back to the front entrance. Walking by the crowds of people I hear them muttering as I pass. I ignore them and focus on my duty. When I get to the front door I order the squads to disperse. I keep the princess and Ash close to the door in case they have to make a run for it. Sam and Markus come up to me.

"This is like those stories we read about! The brave last stand at the palace. Never thought i'd be a part of those stories." Sam glances over to Markus.
"You probably thought you'd be one of those dashing rouges who always finds himself with a warm drink and warmer company." We all laugh. For just a moment we are the bright eyed youths who joined the Combined Arms. Then a crack of a rifle breaks the mood.

Not wasting time I dive behind a crate and look out. Hundreds of people were charging towards us. Their torches made their blades appear crimson in the night. From a glance I can tell they don't have many guns, with so much manpower what's the point? A few people were staying at the back with rifles but most of them had swords, axes, or other crude weapons.

Raising my rifle to my shoulder I pull the trigger and feel the kick as the bullet speeds towards its target. Before it even hits the man i'd aimed at I pulled the bolt back and lined up a shot with another man. Repeating the same process over and over I lose count of the number of bullets I fire.

As the first pirates reach the barricades at the bottom the guards their are quickly overwhelmed and hacked to bits. Reaching into my pockets I find that i'm out of ammo and stand up. Walking towards the oncoming onslaught I see my squad forming up beside me. Taking out a shrapnel grenade the others do the same and as one we throw them into the oncoming enemy.

Ten grenades going off at once creates a large explosion that would probably create a small crater in the marble stairs. That would probably kill a fair amount of the bastards These grenades were made for the singular purpose of sending as much shrapnel in as large a area as possible. The pirates ethier don't know or care about the grenades but when they go off they have a brief moment to regret their life choices.

One moment there's a small army of pirates charging up the steps of the palace, then there's a ear splitting boom. Shrapnel fills the air and as bits of metal find their mark men and woman fall from a hundred wounds. Many are killed instantly from ethir the force of the explosion or from being pierced by shrapnel. They are the lucky ones.

Several people now lay screaming in pain. Men, woman, sprawled out on the stairs with varying degrees of injuries. The lightest of them had only light cuts but some of them were bleeding from deep cuts across their bodies. What made it worse was the sudden end of the fight. The few pirates left on the stairs seemed stunned and the guards and Ash's squad have stopped firing.

I look around me and see that my squad was staring at the enemy as they cry out in pain. Looking at them I feel some disgust but I shrug it off. We may have stopped the assault but their captain remained. After a second of looking around trying to find her I hear clapping from behind me.

Turning around I see the red coated woman with a sword at the throat of the king. She stares at me.
"Are you a well trained warrior or a mad dog?" I pull out a smoke grenade. If i'm lucky she won't be able to tell it's just a smoke.
"Can I be both?" She smiles. Probably not good that I can now say I made a notorious pirate smile.
"A sense of humor on a battlefield? Regardless you really ruined my plans here. I figured you'd have left with your ships, but here you are killing my temps." I look around me at the dead and dying.
"Temps? That's how you view your men? I felt no pity when I killed them but if your their leader I just did them a mercy." Her smile turns into a grin.
"In a way. Regardless i'm on a schedule so if you'd kindly put down your weapons." The royal guards and the princess looked disgruntled and angry but dropped their weapons.

I see how this scum planed things now. Distract us all long enough to sneak in and take the king hostage. So long as she had him she could do whatever she wanted. Hell she could order the guards to carry the islands treasury to her ship and they'd be forced to do it. These 'temps' are the only thing that confuse me. Where did she find so many desperate idiots to do her bidding?

Regardless of how she acquired her resources my path was clear. I am a soldier of Blade, I can not willingly surrender my weapons to some pirate. Besides there was no way we could be sure that she wouldn't just kill him after she was done. She really has put me in an awkward position. She was waiting for me to lower my weapons and I don't think she'd let one of us move to get a clear shot on her.

Smiling I stare into her crimson eyes.
"I'll pass on surrendering my honor to some scum." Her smile dippens a bit.
"I see. Your honor is to kill a king of an allied island. I'm sure your king will be happy to hear how you let another ruler die by the hands of some 'scum'." I finger the pin of the grenade.
"Who said i'd let some scum kill him?"
Her smile completely fades from her face. In its place is a emonsiless mask that hid all expressions.
"You wouldn't." My smile turns into a predatory grin. She looks me up and down before a matching grin grows on her own lips. "I challenge you to a duel then."

What? I can only guess that thought went through every one of my squadmates heads at the same time. Duels are a fast way to deal with problems of honor but a pirate has none so why would she offer? I can't help but shake my head at her absurdity.
"Why would I duel you?" She moves her sword closer to the kings neck.
"Way I see it if I beat you in a duel your men will be free to surrender to me. After all they can't say scum killed a sgt of such an elite force now can they? And before you question my honor, I can't really double cross you if i'm dead."
My best option really.
"Very well. If I win and your still alive you can expect a nice long life in a hole in the ground back home. And if you beat me I doubt my squad will stop you from leaving."

She doesn't know about Steel. Even if I lose here she'll get caught by the captain long before she can get away. As far as I can see this was a win-win.

Taking out my sword I feel my instincts scream a warning. Trusting my senses I duck and roll just as a bullet passes where my head was a moment ago. While my squad turns to find the unseen threat I walk towards Jack. She seems disappointed that i'm still alive but her smile comes back quickly.

"I wouldn't get too much closer if…" Before she finishes I throw the grenade i'd been holding. It hits her smack in the face and by instinct she releases her grip on the old man to grab her face. The old man takes this chance to break free and hurls himself out of the way.

With him gone I go to slash the crimson captain but am blocked by her sword. She grits her teeth.
"You'll pay for that." She push me off with a surprising amount of strength. Before I can recover she strikes a quick slash at my head and I move it just enough for the blade to merely cut my cheek.

I swing my sword in a wide arc to force her back and give me some room. Instead of jumping back she parries my sword away and thrusts her sword toward my chest. I sidestep but not fast enough as she cuts through my shirt and I feel blood flow over my stomach. Releasing her speed and skill is far above what i'd expected I change tactics. I swing my sword at her head but at the last minute press the trigger that allows the blade to retract.

When our blades meet mine is pushed back into its metal fold and using that I smack her in the face. She staggers back and I lunch a series of quick but heavy blows all over her body and end my assault with a heavy swing at her sword arm. She's unable to parry and I feel her bones give way as the metal cover hammers into her arm.

She screams out in rage and instead of falling to her knees in pain as i'd expect she pulls out a dagger and before I can react plunges it into my side. Grabbing her wrist with my free hand I glare at her as I unfold my blade and thrust it into her chest. Her eyes open wide and her mouth opens into a 'O' shape. Clinging to me she whispers into my ear.

"Well fought."

Releasing her wrist she falls to her knees. Taking my sword out of her chest I see my mark was off. If i'd hit anything vital she's have already died yet even now her eyes shine with life. Doesn't matter, she'll bleed out without aid soon enough. Taking a step back I call over Ash. She arrives with a smile on her face that drops once she sees my bleeding side. She quickly gets out some bandages but I point to Jack.

"Fix her up." Ash looks surprised but she's a soldier. Dropping to a knee she begins the painstaking process of stopping the blood flow. While she does that the princess comes over with some of the guards. One of my squad, seven, comes up and begins bandaging me up without a word.

"Why are you helping the bitch?" I look over to the princess. "I want information. Corpse don't like sharing secrets." She looks like she's about to protest but then stops herself.

"I trust you. If nothing else you and your men have earned that much from me today." I look at the woman feared as bloody Jack.

"Don't worry. She won't be harming anyone again." As the princess goes off to tend to her father I see that Jack is staring at me. Her eyes remind me of Sam whenever she find a math problem that made her think. Whatever occupied Jack's thoughts I can only guess at.

Looking out towards the city I hear gunfire in the distance. The fight goes on but my job is here for the moment. This 'pirate' just seems wrong to me. I'm not sure why but I just can't help but think she's not like the scum I thought her to be.

She's far too skilled to just be a pirate. At some point she was trained by someone who knew what they were doing. That or she's the biggest waste of talent i've seen. Not my problem anymore, I'm sure answers will come to light in her interrogation

Chapter 10
Birthday Wish
Jade

8/24/1438

Some people celebrate their birthdays by having a party. Others go about their day like it was any other. I find myself in a lavish ballroom watching as people dance with their partners. While they have their fun i'm forced to shake hands with old men who just want to get in good with my father. At least none of them have tried to get me married to some prince, perhaps I have Daniel to thank for that.

As i'm thinking that I look over to my father and see him talking with king Robert. The kind old man had come with his daughter Sam to show his thanks for Blades efforts on the border. When I had met him he came off like a grandfather figure. My father seems to like him at any rate but his daughter was far more interesting. She stood alone at the edge of the party in a simple blue dress without a care in the world. Like me she seemed to want to leave as soon as possible.

Excusing myself I head over to her. She gives me a pleasant enough smile but I could tell she was wondering why i'd disturbed her.
"You look like your being held here against your will. What'd the dignitaries say if they found out?" I say the last part with a grin on my face and she nods.
"I had the feeling you liked this party as much as me. To be blunt I came here to see a friend." I look around.

"Where are they?" She glances over to a table with drinks. I could see several men and women in uniform as well as a few nobles from other islands. Before I turn back to Samantha I see a familiar face break away from the table with a drink in both hands.

Sgt Conner Green was in full uniform as he walked around people dancing. His dress uniform had gathered some new additions and I recall my father talking about them a while back. On his chest he now wore three red dots that looked like wax had fallen there and been left to dry. Those were the red badges that showed its wearer had received wounds in the line of duty. Getting one meant you saw combat and have a scar to prove it. Getting three meant you were ethir reckless or brave. Regardless how others saw them soldiers all seem to agree they'd rather not get the award.

More interesting was the crimson dagger under his three badges. The blood red dagger was the size of a pen and was a testament to its wearers skill with blades. As guns became more and more advance the medel became harder and harder to get. When dad had said multiple ones had been awarded I never thought Conner would be one of them.

When he gets to us he hands a glass of wine to Samantha and gives a polite bow to me.
"Princess, and princess." He bows again to Samantha but in a more mocking gesture. Even i'm taken back a bit since such a thing was huge insult. I half expect Sam to pour her drink over his head but instead she laughs.
"What took you so long sgt? I nearly died of thirst waiting for you." He takes a sip from his own glass before responding.
"Sorry Sam. Pushing past people who can get me

courtmarshaled made it a little hard." Samantha's smile is warm and honest. A very different one from what she showed me. Taking a step back i'm stopped as Samantha looks over to me.

"Conner you should go get your princess a drink as well. Wouldn't do for her to go thirsty on her birthday." What...

"You got it Sam. What'd you like your highness?" I'm taken by surprise and ask for whatever he had. As he heads off Samantha turns to me.

"We don't have long till he gets back. In the meantime why don't you tell me what you know about him." I blink a couple times.

"You mean Conner?" She nods.

"Of course. I've been talking to him a bunch since he saved my father, but he's never talked much about his family. Kinda made me curious." Oh. I guess someone who's not from Blade wouldn't know.

"His family has served mine longer than we've had the crown. He's the first to not serve in the royal guard so that may be why he wouldn't want to talk about it." She nods.

"So he's a black sheep. I knew I liked him for a reason." I smile, but before I can respond I see him come back with another glass. His hands go to hand it to me but a red gauntlet stops him.

Samantha stares at the guard who seemed to come out of the shadows, but the look Conner gives could melt steel. He looks at his uniform where a couple drops of wine landed.

"You don't really think i'd poison her do you red?" The red armor goes to grab the glass but before he does Conner downs it. After a minute he whistles. "Man that was good. A real shame you wasted some of it on my jacket." I can hear a growl from inside the armor. I knew CA's and royal guards were rivals but never saw the two ever go at each other.

"Conner why don't you relax." Samantha steps in. Conner looks at her a moment before nodding.

"Your right. Can't let a fancy tin can spoil the night." His comment gets another growl out of the guard. Before anything else can come of it another guard comes over and whispers something to the other. They both leave towards my father who seems to be talking with Daniel.

"What was that about?" Samantha is looking after the two guards.

"Their just doing their job, just a little to well." Conner is still glaring at the guard who stopped him. I turn to him.

"I don't understand how two groups who say they serve Blade can hate eachother so much." Conner looks down to the floor. He seems like a kid who got caught in the cookie jar. He opens his mouth but before he can speak I hear my father.

"Ladies and gentlemen! It would appear that my guards have come up with some entertainment for us. They've arranged for a duel to showcase the skills of the men and women who've been fighting off the pirate menace up North." I look at Conner. He has a rather grim smile. "Will both parties from the Combined Arms and the royal guard come to the center."

As Conner goes off to the center the dancing couples break up and form a ring. He was joined by several others in matching uniforms as well as ten royal guards. I head over to my father with Samantha who is looking at Conner with some concern. Getting to my father I grab him by the shoulder.

"What are you doing?" He looks surprised.

"What?" I point towards the ring of people circling Conner

and a royal guard.

"Why the hell are you having them fight?" He looks over to Daniel.

"Remember what you wished for?" What?

I think back to a couple days ago. My father had told me I needed to make a wish for my birthday. He wanted to make sure he'd have enough time to get it ready. All i'd asked for was to go to the academy next year. The academy was a island where future rulers, scientist, and military leaders went to learn from the best the Alliance could give. Every island got a select number of spots a year and I wanted to go to have a taste of the outside world.

It'd be perfect. I'd get to get away from royal guards following me around all the time and i'd get to talk to my peers without a bunch of old people watching us. But I don't see how that relates to Conner fighting a royal guard.

"You don't think we'd let you go off without guards? The Combined Arms and royal guard both want the spot and they agreed to show me which one is best for the job." I glare at him. The bastard not only wants me under guard even at school but is having people fight for the job.

I'm about to say something when a flash of steel catches my eye. Turning around I see the royal guards and CA's in the ring have drawn training swords. They all look ready to kill each other except Conner. He's smiling like this is all just a show.

In a flash one of the guards runs at Conner. His comrades charge behind him and all of them run headlong towards Conner and his squad. Instead of meeting them Conner and his men get into a defensive stance and wait. When the first guard reaches Conner he raises his sword into the air and moves to smash it into Conner's head.

Conner doesn't drop his smile as he steps to the side and uses his sword like a bat and whacks the guard in the side of the head. A loud clang is heard and the guard falls to his knees. As he does two other CA's hit him in the sides with the handles of their swords. In just a few seconds a proud member of the royal guard was lying on the ground.

Shocked from seeing a royal guard so easily taken down I almost miss another one smack the sword away from a CA. The guard proceeds to punch the unarmed man hard enough to knock him on his back. When he raises his sword to finish the man off another CA jumps on his back. The guard struggles with the man and with his attention off the other the CA jumps off. They both begin dueling with their swords and I look around for Conner.

I find him strangling a guard while another is about to strike him in the back with their sword. Insead of hitting Conner back the guard finds his blad locked with another. While the two duke it out behind him Conner chokes out the guard he was fighting. He turns to look around and then runs towards a guard who is pummeling a CA into the ground.

He slams into the guard and they both go down. The guard gets up first and looks over to Conner who's nursing his side. Getting up the guard goes over to Conner as he gets up. Before Conner can get to his feet a swift kick sends him down. The guard goes to kick him again but is stopped when several CAs tackle him. He's brought to the ground from the sheer weight of the others and falls to the ground.

Looking around it was clear the royal guard had been outmatched by the Combined Arms superior squad tactics. I imagine all the guards will be getting a refresher course on unit cohesion. For now through guards came in to carry their comrades off. While they did the CAs surrounded Conner. It was clear he had taken an injury but he waved them away after a minute.

As one they all got up and formed into a single line to bow towards us. Even after getting kicked around Conner still had a grin on his face. Did he enjoy this?

"Well done! Everyone give a hand to our entertainers for their hard work." Everyone applauded. As far as their concerned this was all an act to showcase their skills.

"You should get to know your future classmates Jade." I give my father a glare before heading over to Conner with Samantha. Getting closer I can see one of a man massaging his side.

"I'd say two bruised and maybe one broken." Conner looks at the man and shrugs.

"Guess dancing is out of the question." Another man puts his hand on his shoulder.

"Dancing may be out of the question, but no one will judge you for having a couple more drinks." A woman sighs behind the two as the rest of them laugh. They seemed close, unlike the royal guards who never talked to each other this was refreshing.

"I hear you all will be going to the academy with us." Samantha goes up to them and joins the group. They all seem comfortable with her so it's safe to assume they've spent some time together. Conner looks at the others and then at

Samantha.

"I think you should get your hearing checked. We're still stationed up North." Samantha looked over to me and I smiled.

"Well your king say your going to be my guards while I attend classes." All of them stiffen at the news. Two of them put their hands on on Conner's shoulders to comfort him. His injuries must be more serious than what I heard.

"I see. Well your highness I would recommend another squad to guard you. In fact i'd recommend you take the royal guards." Samantha was looking at all of them.

"You guys didn't know why you were fighting did you?" Conner looks at the others before shrugging.

"We were told the king had wanted a demonstration of what we've learned. It was suggested this would be done best by kicking a bunch of red ass." The others smile or grin, but Conner is looking at me.

"There's no mistake. Your all going to the Academy." As my father turns up Conner and his squad all stand at attention.

"My lord! If those are your orders we shall follow them to the letter." Father nods as he looks Conner over.

"Your squads come to my attention a couple of times now. Captain Steel recommended you to join our souther forces." Conner and his men all flushed with pride.

Blade had four theaters where our forces could be deployed. The West had always been the less desirable option since it was just garrison duty on ships. The North was a good place for fresh troops most of the time since fighting pirates and keeping track of the feds keep life interesting. The East was a tense post at the best of time. Naval skirmishes break out constantly and the possibility of invasion from the Imperium was a constant threat.

The South was different. Seven years ago the explorers found a huge landmass far bigger than any recorded island. Along with Verbun and Alleato, Blade laid claim to the new lands. Around the same time our explorers ran into settlers from the Imperium. The land is far to bountiful to be given up by ethir side and so the place has been split between the Imperium, and the three Alliance members.

Over the years both sides expanded their presence by building forts and trenches around naval bases. At the moment there are only four actual colonies. One from each island laying claim. While the colonists built their homes and explored the lands the military patrolling disputed areas. Saying the place was volatile was an understatement.

Not only were navies fighting at sea the disputed areas is home to a ground war. Both sides are fighting over the land as fast as it's discovered but the Alliance refused to offer support unless the Imperium declared war. The Imperium in response was sending ground forces into disputed areas to assert their claims.

Blade sent their own forces to deny them and fighting broke out. It started as small skirmishes between squads but quickly turned into full blown battles between thousands of soldiers with artillery support. To be sent to the East was to be sent to war, and as far as the soldiers of Blade are concerned it's the best deployment you could ask for. For that reason the East has the best soldiers Blade has to offer as well as a majority of our naval forces.

"Of course I can't have you guys laying around here for a couple months. If I end up sending you guys East it'll only be for a brief time." Conner and the others nod and I look at them.

They didn't want to go to the academy. They wanted to use the skills they'd worked so hard to master. I'm sure they see guarding me as an unnecessary waste. No, not a waste. They'd just rather be out in the world like me. For a moment a picture of me at their side comes to my mind. I smile at the thought but as far as reality is concerned that's wishful thinking.

Chapter 11
Kriegsland
Conner

9/07/1438

Looking around I wonder at the beauty of the place. On top of the watch tower I can see over the wooden walls surrounding the growing town of Holzberg. Past the walls are trenches and concrete bunkers. On top of the bunkers stand flak guns ready to shoot down Imperial airships. Past the trenches is a mile of flattened earth with no cover for any would be attacker. Yet despite the obvious presence of man the sprawling forest past the mile of flat land was what I was staring at.

The large trees dwarfed the walls of the town and made it seem as if we were nothing more than ants. Because of how think the forest was it was impossible to see through, even the roads that had been painstakingly cut out by the army could not keep the forest at bay. The smoothed out land had tufts of grass all over it and it seemed as if the trees themselves were moving to cover the road. It was a testament to nature's beauty and to man's determination.

The fact that people had taken the weeks of marching to get to this new town was impressive. To see all that they had done with so little help from the army was truly remarkable. The army may have set up the defensives and the roads, but the people built the homes and plowed the fertile lands behind them. One day this town will be a haven to people exploring these new lands, but for now the people here were settling in.

As I stood watching I could see people walking down the road. If memory serves than those are the explorers that had left before the we arrived. They were supposed to be looking for natural rivers and any other resources that could be useful to a new town. Pulling out a scope I look through it and see the mud caked men and women. They each carried large packs on their backs that seemed to weigh them down slightly.

The man next to me rings a bell a couple of times and as I watch several soldiers line up in the trenches and prepare for battle. Along the ramparts more soldiers man machine guns. With in a minute the whole town was ready to repel an invasion. The soldiers seemed to expect this band of explorers to be the vanguard of an imperial army which I would find humorous if I hadn't been warned that it has happened before.

Apparently a few years back an Imperial raiding party tailed one of our expedition and when the our guard was down they attacked. While I doubt that'll happen so far away from imperial lands I can't say it doesn't pay to be prepared. Besides with so much land I find it hard to believe their aren't natives here. I'd rather our defences were ready in case a army of natives decide to reclaim their lands.

"Sgt Green!" I look down from the watchtower. Standing below was a young man in uniform. "Orders from HQ sir! Your to take your squad to investigate reports of imperials." Heading down the ladder the man hands me a letter. As he heads off I open it and see a set of coordinates and a written version of what the runner had just told me. I look around and see Marcus chatting with a couple smiths. Heading over he sees me and salutes.

The smiths go off and I smile at Markus.
"Get the squad prepped. I want everyone at the front gate in ten minutes."

He nods and runs off to find the others. While he does so I head over the watchtower. At one of it's four legs is a backpack with a rifle. I shift through it real quick to check that everything's in order. Two weeks rations. three weeks water, shovel, shaving kit, knife, one hundred rounds for my rifle, fifty rounds for my side arm, and ten rounds for Gearbox's pistol.

Nodding at everything being where it should be I take out the ten rounds and put them in my new gauntlets. Simple leather that had five loops where it meets my wrist. I put a bullet in each of these loops and tug them a bit to make sure their secure. I had these made before I left for here on a whim and I wonder how useful they'll be.

Grabbing my pack I head over to the front gate. A wooden gate won't do much against modern artillery but it was still effective at stopping infantry and providing at least some cover for the civilians. I see a couple guards looking around. Even through their alert and performing their duties it's clear their bored, as any soldier put on guard duty would be.One of them comes up to me and I hand him my orders. He stares at the metal circle dangling from my neck.

After confirming my identity he nods to the others and they start opening the gate. As they do my squad arrives. Before the gate opens the whole way my squad is fully assembled and ready for combat. It was clear by looking at their faces that they hoped to see action against the Imperium. As their commanding officer I should urge them not to seek combat but I am not a hypocrite. I want to test my metal against the Imperium just as much as they do, perhaps even more.

"Come on lads, we got a date with some imperials."

9/12/1438

Looking around the forest I try to see any signs of human life. Besides the tracks from the the three i'd sent to scout ahead of us there was no sign anyone had been here in the last month, let alone the last week. I shouldn't be so impatient, that's a good way to make mistakes. With some effort I calm myself and continue my survey of my surrounding without haste.

With the sun starting to come down i'm about to call a halt when I hear movement from the front. I assume a kneeling stance with my rifle and prepare to fire but quickly stand when I see it is one of my scouts. As he comes forward he nods towards me and reports in little more than a whisper.

"We found some tracks up ahead. Six sets in close formation heading North East. Judging by the prints i'd say they're a heavy infantry squad."

All of us tense at the mention of heavy infantry. While many thought with the rise of guns the knight would fall out of favor the knights themselves refused to leave the battlefield. Now like the royal guard knights used plate armor that was not only reinforced but also enchanted. The strength of the enchantment varied greatly between knights due to how much they cost as well as by how skilled the enchanter was.

The Alliance and UIA have very few knights and the ones we have are all assigned to their home's defence or as their lord's personal guards. The Confederation had more but that was mainly because they saw knights as a status symbol rather then tools of war. All three of us combined couldn't match the Imperium through. Even going off of official numbers they have tens of thousands of knights. Not only that but the Imperium happily boosted about their knights high levels of enchantment.

While I don't believe the part about their knight being equal to a thousand men I know for a fact that their a threat. If the Imperium has sent in kights they may be getting ready for a large assault or perhaps even a full on invasion. No. If they were here to attack us there'd be more than six, and they'd have light infantry to support them. Also going off where their tracks are heading their going into uncharted lands.

Why would imperial knights be heading into lands that hadn't been charted yet? They could be claiming land for the Imperium but if that was the case they shouldn't have had to pass through our lands. Wait. This should still be our lands, so why haven't we seen any outposts or sentires? And why has such a small number of imperials been allowed to pass? Even if their imperial knights the local outpost should be able to at least repel them.

"Three, where's the closest outpost?" Three takes out a map from her pack and scans it for a few seconds.
"Should be four miles West of us. Another one's ten miles East at the edge of our explored area."

I look at my squad a moment. Nine and ten would be on the trail of the imperials. We need to alert HQ about this but at the same time we need to get confirmation. My squad isn't incompetent but even the best tracker has mistaken prints before. Not only that but I want to know why our outpost didn't intercept. If the imperials came close to one than we shouldn't be getting reports of possible activity.

"Six, seven, and eight. I want you three to head to the outpost. Find out why they didn't see a squad of knights coming through their yard. While your at it send a report to HQ. And if you can manage getting us some help from the outpost I won't complain." They nod and head off. When their gone I look towards the rest of my squad. "New objective. Find out why the imperials are here and how they managed to pass through our grid without being identified." They all nod and together we head after our scouts.

It doesn't take us long to catch up to our scouts. They quickly inform me that the knights are clearly hunting something. Ten had found fresh blood on a tree and horse tracks. Not only that but nine had found a spent casing. He hands it over to me and I look at it while we walk.

This wasn't one of ours. It fits with an older model the army was using until just a couple months ago but they'd been issued new rifles with a lower caliber bullet. The current plan for Blade's R&D department is to move to the new Marksman's rifles that have two operational models currently in use. The M1 is the standard infantries choice while snipers used the M2. CA command had been offered the new rifles but had declined to make it standard kit until it met their own high standards.

So why would a casing from a now outdated rifle be here? I would understand if some soldiers placed on guard duty had the old model rifle but all the troops on the border should have the newest rifles in abundance. In the distance I hear shots being fired. Putting the casing in my pocket I ready my rifle. With a wave of my hand the squad moves into a wide formation and we advance.

The closer we get the louder the sounds of combat become. Isolatonting the sounds of gunfire in my mind I can't make out any of the new rifles in the fight. Getting closer I make out a couple men in the uniform of Blade as well as one in a Verbun uniform. Alarm bells start going off in my head.

The defense plan had taken into account how moral is increased when soldiers are fighting with people from their own islands. So while the main front with the imperium where skirmishes break out several times a week has divisions from all three islands the rest of the defensives try to keep the units separated. This area was under Blades jurisdiction, and to my knowledge no call for aid had been issued to other units. It may be possible that a nearby unit came to help one of ours but two things put their identity into question. One: they are clearly in a full encirclement of their enemy which is against protocol to say the least. Two: With at least two units we should of heard or seen some of their members watching out for flanking forces. Moving closer I try and get a look at what their shooting at.

My eyes widen in shock as I see the shining plated armor of the knights. They were arrayed in a circle with large shields providing cover from the incoming fire. In their formation they couldn't attack but it was clear the soldiers here couldn't break through the enchanted metal of their shields. Painted on their shields is the black eagle of the imperial royal family. These were not just imperial knights, they were in the service of a member of the imperial royal family.

Coming up behind one of the men in a Blade uniform I tap his shoulder. He turns with a cry and curses in a language i'm not familiar with. Before he can raise his rifle to shoot me I slap it away and slam his head into the tree he had been using as cover. He crumples to the ground and before the rest of his friends can react my squad takes them out in short order. Looking over to the mussel flashes I can just make out soldiers in the last rays of light. Taking the unconscious man's rifle I raise it and pull the trigger. A man in a Blades uniform falls over clutching at his chest.

With surprise on our side we kill several of them before they relise whats up. A couple shots land near me and I lean into a tree for cover. Taking out a smoke grenade I pull the pin and toss it towards the knights. It takes a couple seconds but soon they are obscured by smoke, and then the whole clearing is nothing but white clouds. With a smokescreen they make their way towards us and as they get near the attention the imposters had been giving me stops. Popping up from my cover I get ready to return fire but find no targets. I wait for them to reappear but nothing happens.

After several minutes of tense silence I look towards the rest of my squad and the knights. The knights were looking at us and probably wondering if we're friends while my squad was searching the dead and securing the wounded. I toss aside the rifle i'd taken earlier and head over to the knights. They tense up but I raise my hands.

"Hey i'm not sure what your doing here or what's going on,

but I think you guys can give me some answers." The knights look to each other and begin speaking in the imperial tongue. I had learned a little but it was limited to demanding surrender and swear words. After a few minutes one of them gets ahead and nods towards me.
"You in charge?" Her words are drenched in a thick accent.
"Sgt Green, these are my men. I want to know why the hell you're so deep in OUR lands."

Several of the knights raise their shields and some of them place their hands on the pommels of their swords. In response my squad raise their rifles and aim at the joints of the knights armor. At nearly the same time me and the knight who'd spoken to me raise our arms and tell our men to stand down. We stare at each other for a moment before she speaks.

"We were chasing a group that attacked one of our border forts. We believe their responsible for several civilian expeditions that have gone missing." I shake my head.
"I won't say we don't do raids, but I doubt it was any of ours if they attacked from here." She looks at me for a moment.
"And why should I belive you?" I take out my rifle and hand it over to her.
"You'll find it's design is a bit different from the ones that they were using. That's because we upgraded our weapons recently. As to why we wouldn't raid you here, we're setting up our own fortifications at the moment and don't have plans for offensives in this sector."

She looks at me for a moment, trying to see any lies or half-truths in my words. It's true we upgraded our weapons and it's also true we won't be going on the offensive here anytime soon. The reason though isn't because we're building fortifications. This sector is still new and they just finished the towns defences Aside from that all we have here is an early warning system that's job is to buy the army time to withdraw as many civilians as possible. But i'm not about to let imperials know that.

"So why is it there were no defence forces stopping us? If these are not your forces we were tracking than where are yours? Surly they'd have come to investigate." I point to myself.
"And what do you think our job is? We came from a base nearby that is wondering if your a vanguard for an invasion." She laughs for a moment, and I find myself taken by surprise.
"What's so funny?" She stops laughing but I sense there's a smile under that helmet.
"You think we're invading? No we've only been here for a few months to set up a town. The only thing we're invading is the local fauna." I stare at her a minute.
"So a squad of imperial knights under the service of the royal family is setting up a town?" She looks at me for a moment as her laughter begins to die down.
"Is it your business to question the imperial family?" I tap the badge on my cap.
"Well if the imperial family has some of it's knights in lands under Blade then it is in fact my business." The slits in her visor seem to eye me up and down. Whatever had her in a joyous mood is clearly gone.
"I don't suppose you'll just let us go huh?" I look at them.

I find her asking this question rather stupid. Her six knights vs my seven CAs. Even if she wasn't holding my rifle the odds would be stacked against me. If a fight broke out my best chance is to run and hope their too tired to give chase. Perhaps it's not the noblest of actions but it's the only one that doesn't end with seven caps resting on rifles.

"If you'll accept an escort me and my men will see you to your lands. If possible i'd like to stop by a outpost on the way to report that your not an invasion force. Be awkward if a couple divisions came all the way out here for nothing." The knights behind their leader get a little stiff. Enchanted armor or no a division is more than enough to overrun them.
"If that's the case we'd be very appreciative of the escort."

She hands me back my rifle and I order the squad to move out. We form a semi circle around the knights in case we run into any observers. Better that they see knights under guard then beside us. Before we head out I look over to the man i'd slammed into a tree and find three shaking her head. Guess I had hit him harder than I thought. A shame, a prisoner could have answered a lot of questions.

The outpost is only a hour or so away so we press on but it's clear we won't be getting the knights out of our lands today. With night upon us we travel closer together and our pace is slowed greatly. After what seems like a lifetime we finally see lights from a building.

Following standard procedure I take out a flashlight and raise it up so that an observer can see me. The rest of my squad does the same and soon we're all illuminated for the sentires to see. The knights seem uncomfortable but considering the circumstances that can't be avoided.

"One!" I see someone running towards us. I recognize him as ten. He stops short as he sees the knights but quickly recovers and salutes me. "We got problems here boss." I glance at the knights who have tensed up.

"What's wrong ten?" He shakes his head.

"It'd be easier to tell you what's right. When we got here we found the garrison dead and their equipment either smashed or stolen. Eight and nine managed to get the lines working and reported to HQ, but apparently several of our outposts have gone dark. Seems like an imperial invasion is on it's way." He looks over to the knights. They look at each other before their leader speaks up.

"We are not invading. That said I believe it's important for us to get to our side of the border quickly." They all seem full of energy suddenly. They were going home tonight.

I should stop them, but I know we can't stop them. Just taking a glance at the others I can tell their thinking the same. Duty can be a real pain. With some reluctance I point it at the knight's face. The others do the same and I see the knights raise their shields.

"I'm afraid i'm gonna ask you to wait until I can confirm there's no invasion. I ask you to come quietly." She stares at me for a moment before raising her shield.

"I'm sorry, but we can't wait." She says something else in her native tongue. Before they charge I open fire with the rest of my squad. Bullets fall on the knights like rain and just like rain it does nothing.

While firing I slowly back off to get more distance. We've trained for this, through we all knew it was more to delay then actually win. The knights take their abuse for a couple minutes before we have to reload. Once we given them a respite they charge.

I lose track of the others as their leader races towards me. She tries to slam her shield into me but I sidestep and hit her in the head with the butt of my rifle. The solid wood makes and audible crack as it meets the plated metal of her helmet. I can see the splinters spread through the wood and while she staggers back it's clear that's all the damage she took.

Weak points for a knight were all the same. The joints and the head. No matter what you did you couldn't keep either completely protected. In this case I didn't even dent her helm, but the force of my blow hopefully dazed her slightly. Taking advantage I use the rifle as a club and smack the back of her shield. This forces her to open her guard and I quickly stab my rifle down towards her knee, aiming for the joint between the plates.

Before I can see if the 'aim for the joints' works her right hand shoots out and grabs my rifle. Using her shield she shoves me back, giving her time to recover. Drawing my side arm in my left hand I take out gearbox's pistol in my right. Surveying the fight real quick I see four and six on the ground not moving and two getting thrown into a tree. Three is beating on a knight with her sword but as I watched the blade shattered and the knight rose. Before the knight can attack three I shoot their back six times. It distracts them long enough for three to get some distance. From there she draws her own sidearm and shoots the knight in the side.

"Don't forget me!" I jump back as a shield slams into the ground where I was. Looking at the knight I holster my side arm and aim gears pistol at her. She rushes me with her shield raised high. I wait until she's point blank and fire. The deafening boom echoes throughout the night. The shot slams into the knight's shield and in slow motion I see her fall back in surprise from the force of the blast. In that moment I grab a bullet from my wrist and put it into the chamber. Closing in she braces the shield to protect her body and head but I aim for her leg instead. She tries to correct her mistake but it's too late.

As my finger pulls the trigger I feel something heavy slam into my side. My body goes flying and I slam into the ground a couple feet away. I feel a sharp pain in my side when I try to get up and know i've broken a rib or two. Not far from me I see my gun and I crawl towards it. Before I reach it a hand grabs my leg and pulls me back. As i'm lifted into the air I grab a smoke and pull the pin.

I hear a gasp of surprise and i'm dropped to the ground. Feeling the sharp pain shoot through my body I can't stop a cry of pain from leaving my lips. I toss away the smoke grenade and look around me. My squad is laying all around, nine and eight had come to our aid and both were slumped up against a tree now. I feel a surge of anger flow through my body and with it an influx of energy.

Getting up I ignore the pain in my side and run towards my gun. A knight makes to stop me but I sidestep them and slash them with my sword. The blade immediately snaps off, but i'm able to reach my new favorite gun. Picking it up I aim at the knight and fire. This one didn't have the experience to know to block and takes the shot head on.

Unfortunately i'm outside of it's effective range so instead of punching a hole in their chest it just knocks the wind out of them. Quickly I reload and run over o finish them off. I'll make sure one of them dies with us. Pointing the gun at their head I suddenly all my strength leave my body. Looking down I see a sword in my side. I should be feeling pain or shock but instead all I feel is tired.

The sword leaves my side and I fall to my knees and see the knights gathering around me. I try to raise my pistol but just can't muster the strength. My eyes slowly close and I hear in the distance the knights talking amongst themselves.. I guess this is it then.

Chapter 12
Wake Up Call
Conner

10/03/1438

Opening my eyes I see a bright light. I raise my hand over my eyes and wonder why the afterlife is so damn bright. When my eyes adjust I find myself in a bed near a window. Looking out I see the sun and quickly avert my eyes. Looking to around the room I see a couple chairs and a door.

The afterlife is rather spartan. I also figured my ancestors would be here to greet me at least. Ancestors? Your decedent has come to the next life! I wonder if their out to lunch. Speaking of lunch i'm hungry. Wait. If i'm dead then why am I hungry? Do I have to worry about eating in the afterlife too? That sucks.

The door opens and a man in a lab coat comes in with a metal pan. He stops as he sees me and I raise my hand to say high when he rushes over and grabs my head. He looks into my eyes and then asks me something in a language that sounds familiar....Shit.

I'm not dead. I've been captured. This is great. Just...great. Ancestors I apologize for my earlier disrespect and hope you'd find it in your hearts to forgive me. I'm sure the afterlife is very nice and not stupid at all.

The man who I assume is a doctor seems happy at least. He's smiling and nodding to himself and after poking and prodding me for a bit he cheerily walks out of the room. I look under the blanket and see i'm naked and that there's a pan that smells like crap. Well I guess there is a good reason for that. I test myself and manage to get sit up.

My limbs feel so heavy. It's like they weigh an extra ten pounds. Not to mention they seem to move slower then I remember them. Did they drug me? No it's likely due to a long period of rest. I must of been out of it for a while. Attempting to get up I nearly fall over but manage to stop myself.

I slowly make my way to the door and look out. I see a open room with a couple people milling about. The doctor from earlier is talking to a couple people at a desk. What catches my eyes is one of the knights from the forest. Their looking at the conversion when they turn my way. I quickly close the door and head over to the window.

Opening it I immediately jump out without a thought for my own wellbeing. My face promptly slams into dirt and I realize I was on the ground floor. Getting up I notice people staring at me. In a split second i'm running. I make it a couple of steps before I stumble and crash into the ground again. Man I must of been out of it for awhile.

Getting up I continue my run at a more measured pace. A couple imperial soldier block my path with confused looks on their faces and I reach for my sword. Feeling nothing but my own flesh I remember i'm naked and therefore don't have a sword. The guards bow their head in my direction and turning around I see the knight. Before I can act they grab my arm like i'm some sort of child and start dragging me back to the building.

I give up at resisting since fighting a knight in the nude just seems wrong. Also even if by some miracle I won those soldiers would gun me down. My only real option is to be dragged around until I get a chance to escape.

When we get back to the building the other people there stare at me in a mixture of curiosity and amusement. If I had a sword I bet they wouldn't be smirking. As i'm thinking this thought i'm shoved back into my room. This time the knight comes in after me and stands by the window. I guess their not interested in chasing me down again but I wonder why they don't just put me in a room without a window. Maybe one with bars and chains just to make sure I can't run away.

After a couple minutes a man comes in and drops off some robes. He starts talking in their language again but the knight cuts him off. He looks at the knight and then to me before nodding and heading out. Did he expect a foreign soldier to know their language? I may know one or two of the languages the Confederation uses but as far as the Imperium goes I can just shout swear words. Really should of taken the time to learn it.

Putting on the robes I find them rather comfy. They reach to my ankles and a sash makes sure nothing is at risk of showing. Besides from that it just feels nice. Whatever fabric that it's made of is really soft and makes me feel like i'm on a cloud. What is going on?

I glance over to the knight standing guard over the window. I'm a prisoner, so why am I getting nice clothing? To my knowledge it's expected under the laws of war that prisoners are given a spare uniform or set of clothes to wear but this is a bit fancy for a prisoner. Not only that but besides the knight there was no one guarding me. There should of been at least two guards in here at all times and if a window was unavoidable then another two out there.

"I guess you're wondering what's going on." I look over to see a woman with short brown hair. She is wearing a robe like mine but with fine embroidery all over. Aside from her dress the real odd thing was her eyes. They were the color of gold and i'd never heard of someone with golden eyes. "Something the matter?" She's frowning in my direction. I shrug.

"Getting stabbed tends to put me in a bad mood." Her golden eyes glance to where I was stabbed. I place a hand there as if to check to make sure there wasn't a sword still in there.

"Your injury was an unfortunate accident. I had hoped to just render your unit unable to hinder our return, but well…" I glare at her. Her voice should of tipped me off. She's the leader of the knights.

"Yeah. Accidents like this happen all the time! I remember how I accidently killed those guys who were attacking you. Real mistake that." Her frown deepens.

"If you hadn't then the imperial army would be marching through your lands right about now. So if anything consider this whole thing a misunderstanding. One that's going to work well for all of us." I look around the room a moment.

"Yup. Alway wanted to be a prisoner of war. I've always wondered if the food for pows was any good." At the mention of food a loud rumble begins emitting from my stomach. She glances over to the knight.

"Could you go and bring us some food please?" The knight nods and heads out. Once she's gone the woman begins looking me up and down. "I've been reading up on you. You guys don't like advertising individual accomplishments do you? All I could find on you was you were a part of the unit assigned to Water when Jack attacked it, but as far as what you yourself have done we can only guess. Personally I think your too skilled not to have some decorations." I shrug.

"I'm a soldier of Blade. That's all i'm required to tell you under the laws of war." She smirks a bit.

"Good thing we're not at war then. No need to hide your accomplishments here." Before I can answer the knight comes back with a tray. She lays it on the bed and I go over to it.

The tray is filled with cups full of rice and meat. From the smell i'd say the meat was fish. I pick up a fork and one of the bowls of rice. She does the same and we both start eating in silence. I had rice a couple times at Water, but this tasted better somehow. Finishing it I take a bowl of meat and begin eating. The taste confirms that it's fish and well prepared as well. Fish was something I'd grown tired of over the past year. Considering how hungry I am I forget that and enjoy the food.

After we finish we look at each other for a moment until I break the silence.

"Do you mind explaining things to me? Feels like a lot has happened." She nods.

"Quite a lot has happened. You see I am princess Mary. I'm fourth in line for the throne and was given the task of leading the colinasion project here. After reviewing the situation I was contemplating working out a treaty with the Alliance to split the island. Unfortunately several expeditions began disappearing around here and it was believed the Alliance was responsible. At first I sent a military patrol to search for them but when they disappeared I decided to deal with this personally. Not far into our journey we engaged with some horsemen. We killed two of them and one run off. After giving chase we were ambushed and you came to our timely rescue. From there you know what happened but when we learned about your garrison being killed we feared it may of been a plot to force our two people to war. After our fight we took your men into your outpost and then brought you with us to get medical treatment." I think for a moment before responding. The weight of her words demand that I take this seriously.

Normal people would see war as wasteful, and in most cases that'd be true. In this case however the Imperium declaring war would be a boon. Blade, **Verbun and** Alleato were already digging in for a war here. We were practically fighting one already on certain fronts. But if the Imperium declares war that means they intend to invade our home islands. In that case the Alliance has to defend us or risk the entire faction crumbling. If you can't expect aid when you need it then why be together in the first place.

"You have any idea who might want you dead?" She shrugs. "I may not be the next in the line for the throne but i've got plenty of influence. Influence has a tendency to attract jealousy, so it's less who wants me dead and who also wants a war." I nod slowly. That makes sense.

Thinking about it'd make the most sense it was someone from our side but then why all the cloak and dagger? If we knew a imperial princess was here and where to find her than killing her would be easy. We'd just lunch a raid with some light artillery. Not only would that get the same results but it'd do it without having our garrisons killed. I relay my thoughts to her and she nods.

"I doubt it's from your side. We should find out more after the treaty is signed next month." I raise an eyebrow.
"Treaty?" She smiles.
"Yes. I've been working on getting terms for these new lands since I arrived and after this incident I managed to strike an agreement. The treaty will have us share these lands by joint exploration. Once a year we'll come together to decide who should get the newly discovered lands. It also covers trade agreements and some other insurances for peace." I nod slowly.
"So… What insurances did you put in place?" Her smile turns to a grin. I think this is what a mouse feels like when a cat wants to play.
"Well you did impress me and my knights. Even after your entire squad was defeated you not only kept fighting but nearly killed one of us. Add to that how much trouble you gave me before you drew that pistol of yours. We in the Imperium pride ourselves in our combat prowess and we like to improve ourselves. So I made sure to include time for you to teach us your technique in the time before the treaty." I shake my head.
"Sorry but i'm not going to…" She cuts me off by handing me a letter. After reading it I can confirm my new orders are to be a good 'guest' for the princess. They specifically mention training whoever she deems fit as well as making clear not to piss them off. If it wasn't written in code and bearing the CA seal i'd call it a fake.

"Very well. I'll see about training tomorrow." She smiles again.
"Looking forward to it."

Chapter 13
The New Deal
Lora

11/11/1438

Reading the new treaty I have to say i'm impressed. This princess Mary was smart. Not only has she guaranteed an easy territorial gain for her people but put a halt to hostilities. She's saved hundreds if not thousands of lives, yet I have to wonder what she gets out of this.

With the plan to have joint expeditions to scout out the lands we'll be able to map the new land significantly faster. Agreeing to meet up once a year to split the lands up also insures we won't have any more skirmishes over disputed lands. It also means a fair split of the lands, at least on paper. Of course it'd be irresponsible to assume this princess is as sincere as she says. After all she did strong arm us into allowing Conner to train her and her personal knights.

Thinking about not only the secrets of the CA's but also the Greens makes my blood boil. Even if it was only a month it'd be foolish to think that they haven't learned something. I guess I should be at least a little thankful. If they wanted they could of just kept Conner's survival a secret and forced the information out of him. At least this way they don't learn all of our secrets and he's limited only to teaching them personnel combat.

Really I should be like the rest and just be happy he's even alive. When the report that his squad went silent after reporting contact with imperial knights had grim implications. Finding nine out of ten of them alive if not beaten up was considered a miracle, but it wasn't lost on us who was missing. Sargent Conner Green; CA, Green, future student of Independence academy.

Intelligence had wanted a squad of CA's deployed on a kill/rescue mission before they broke his will. I'd was shocked at how ready father was to approve it but Daniel speaking up had spooked everyone. I had thought he was going to scold the others for abandoning a comrade, not to mention his own son, but instead he said it'd be best to drop the rescue thing entirely. He mentioned that no one could confirm he was even alive and if he was then he'd kill himself before he betrayed his king. For that reason there was no point risking more lives for one that was probably already lost.

I had excused myself after that and even after hearing about the treaty and Conners survival I haven't been able to look at Daniel the same way. How could he so cously throw away any chance for his son? Did he not care? Yet even Daniel's cold demeanor was only the second worst thing to happen in a day. I still remember telling Samantha over the phone that Conner was MIA and presumed dead.

I had felt a strong need to do something and the only thing I could think of was to inform our mutual friend. She offered all the support Water could give. Said Conner was a hero there and they'd be damned if they didn't at least get something to bury.

When the treaty came we were surprised. The terms were fair and hearing that Conner was alive if not injured was a relieve.

The terms were easy to sign off on for my father but I was focused on the fact that Conner was alive. Samantha had been overjoyed but was concerned about his injury. I shared this concern and agreed with her when she said she'd only be satisfied when she sees him in person.

Daniel took a couple days off so that he can see Conner home when he gets back. He probably feels guilty for abandoning him to his fate. I hope by spending time with his son he'll grow to appreciate what he almost lost. Perhaps he'll not be so quick to abandon him the next time he's listed as MIA.

I feel a chill run up my spine. Next time. Conner is a soldier and while things have quieted down recently that doesn't mean they'll stay that way. CA's are the first ones we throw at problems and in the last year they've been thrown into the spotlight. Taking out Jack caused a lot of people to wonder about the Combined Arms, and the more they learned the more they praised them.

I inquired to some CA captains how they felt about being in the public eye and they surprised me. Most of them hated it. They didn't like how people were aware of them, said it ruined their element of surprise. They also voiced concerns that they'll be used in more political ways rather than combat. It was clear that they'd rather not be the poster child for the Alliance and they were really concerned that was were things were heading.

I'd thought them paranoid. When my father said he'd been asked by half the Alliance and the council to deploy more CAs I believed that the CAs would be on more than a few posters. It'd be foolish for my father to not send regiments out to earn favor with our allies. And the more their sent out the more the public will see. The more the public sees the more they'll like. At least that's how I imagine it'll go.

I guess there's no point in going over the past. Instead I should focus on the next four years of my life. I'll be learning the inner workings of government and how to manage my own. I'll make contacts that'll help me once I become queen. Or I can just have a lot of fun away from any royal guards. Think i'll enjoy the latter more than any of the others.

Really Blade's royal family has never been too keen on the Academy. We don't trade much due to our self reliance. Anything we make we tend to keep and selling weapons just sounds like a good way to get in trouble. Aside from that none of our people are so inclined to become merchants when they'd rather be soldiers. Even farmers tended to want to become soldiers but refrain from doing so so soldiers can eat.

My mind comes back to the trade part of the treaty. Trading with the Imperium is a hard thing to do. They strictly regulate the whole thing and allow only so many ships at carefully selected ports. The deals they've made are all in their favor and independent trading from island to island is strictly regulated. The Commonwealth has fought three wars to try and get better deals and failed each time. As for the Alliance we have almost no trade with them. The border of our two factions is less than safe for our military let alone unarmed merchant ships.

With the trade deal we could make a nice profit. Since there's a safe port for both our peoples we could trade without worrying about being attacked on 'accident'. Add to the fact that now laws exist for land based trade and the limit on trade is gone. I see. This would make the colonies on both sides rich from trade. That detail escaped me until now but I bet this princess Mary knew what she was doing.

She'll be able to purchase Alliance goods in abundance and then sell them to other islands in the Imperium. This treaty has no doubt skyrocketed her influence as well as filled her purse. Trading with them we should be able to make quite a bit as well and maybe be able to get support for our colonies to expand. We'll have to make sure no one else tries to claim lands there.

The rest of the Alliance will see the benefits soon and will probably not like having us as a middleman. I bet in the next year they'll be wanting to help colonize the lands our soldiers have died to keep. They'll offer support and protection when there's no threat of invasion and a promise of profit. Not on our watch.

I get up and head off to find father. This imperial princess is not the only one that can come up with smart ideas.

Chapter 14
School Boat
Conner

12/20/1438

Looking around I could see our escorts. Fifty-four ships, two from every island in the Alliance. All of them were destroyer class vessels brisling with anti-air defences. No airships had a chance of taking this fleet down and the destroyers could handle themselves against any sea based threat. I guess if we went up against a fleet we'd be in trouble but only the four factions can muster one big enough to threaten us.

"Sargent! You should stop avoiding people and come back to the party." I look over to see who's calling me. Tony or five when we're on mission. He's the teams main medic even through we are all trained in field medicine. I tap my side.
"Last time I went to a party my ribs were almost broken." He nods.
"Yeah I remember. But there's no royal guards on this ship." I smile at that.
"True enough. I still don't want to dance, and unless our squads dropped in popularity in the last ten minutes I doubt people will leave me alone."

The moment we got on board we'd been asked countless times to recite tales of our deeds and whenever there's a party which seems almost daily we always find ourselves being asked to dance. Everyone from nobles to rich kids want to be our friends. Markus seems to be enjoying it but the rest of us would rather have less party time.

This ship was massive and held two hundred and seventy students comfortably. Every student was given their own room which had a bed, desk, and bathroom. The crew was also in great numbers. It seemed every corner hid a waiter or maid ready to serve you. Kinda creepy if you ask me, but since the ship was designed to carry nobles and rich kids I guess I can't be surprised.

"You could just be social. All the others are doing their best to get along with the others." I shrug.
"I know I just...They all feel so young, like kids. Besides that most of them are spoon fed brats who think they know everything." Tony scratches his head at my outburst.
"Your only twenty sir. Most of these 'kids' are only a year or two younger than you. As for the spoon fed bit. Well you're probably right about that. Still you'd be perfect for guarding Jade. She just seems to want to talk with Samantha and Sam want's a break from all the 'girl' talk." I stare at him for a moment.
"So she sent you up here to get me to replace her. I bet she wants to sneak out and hide in the library."

Among the vast number of amenities on the ship they had a library. A vast one with hundreds if not thousands of books that seem to gather dust. Really shouldn't have put those on what is essentially a party boat. Very few of the students actually use it, through my squad have been enjoying it. I myself have read a couple books on strategy and tactics as well as a few history books.
"Very well. I'll head down and relive her." Tony smiles and together we walk down some stairs and through a couple corridors until we reach the ball room. A ridiculously large room with tables, chairs, stadium, hundreds of waiters and

servants, and a seemingly endless number of musicians performing. Several students were dancing in their rather plain school uniforms and I could see a couple people in military dress.

The school had a uniform but allowed members of the military wear their own if they wished. The school's uniform was a dark blue dress jacket with black pants. The girls had the option of a skirt while men were forced to wear ties. I hated ties. Only wear mine for special occasions and somehow it fell in a fire after Jades coming of age party. Real strange that.

Ignoring the students asking to dance or talk as well as the servants wondering if we'd like a drink we manage to find our charge. Jade was talking to Samantha and Sam in a small table while in the distance some men were seeming to get ready to approach. Before they do Sam gives them a look I recall from training. The men quickly turn tail and look for other dance partners. Tony and I then approve and the girls all smile, through Sam's seems rather forced.

She gets up and grabs Tony by the arm and waves at me as she walks away.
"Have fun Romeo." I stare after her.
"Who?" Romeo...I feel like i've heard the name before. Was he a drill instructor? I look to Jade and Sam to ask but they both seem interested in the floor. I see now. Must be some sort of inside joke. Guess they've gotten close during this trip.

Walking over I take Sam's seat. She seemed to be drinking something that smells vaguely like alcohol and I finish it off for her. The others looked at me and I shrugged.

"Wouldn't want it to go to waste." They glance at each other and smile before talking about their courses. Jade is taking course on government, economy and diplomacy. Samantha is taking much the same except she's taking a couple classes in combat and tactics as well.

I'm happy to inform her that we'll be spending some time together. Besides the diplomacy classes where i'm 'guarding' Jade my courses are all more war centered. The one i'm most looking forward to is a new one. The UIA sold a couple of their new single seater airships called planes to us. Blade's still testing it to see how we could incorporate it but ever since i've heard about them i've wanted to try flying one. To think a single person can soar through the heavens, free to go or do whatever they desire.

Shaking my head I return to listening to Jade and Samantha.
"The Confederates have been threatening to increase tariffs."
Jade shrugs.
"Trades not our thing. Speaking of that I wouldn't worry about them. Don't suppose you'd rather send your trade our way?" Samantha's face changes to confusion as she clearly tries to decline without offending. Not surprising since Blade isn't well known for its trade. In fact i'm sure some people don't even know we own trading ships.
"You do know we mainly sell luxury goods like silk and stuff right? I don't see much profit for that for Blade." Jade nods.
"Of course not, but our colonies were hoping to begin trading with the imperials in the next couple weeks. We don't have much to offer except tools and raw materials so I was hoping you'd be willing to give us something to sell to them."
Samantha bliks a couple times before nodding. It's clear she's thinking a mile a minute.

"I see… In that case we could send over a couple ships. How much you willing to pay?" Jade pretends to think for a moment. I can tell she's pretending by how her lips begin to curl into a grin before she speaks again.

"Oh we'll pay what the feds pay but without the tariffs. After all we are friends aren't we?" Samantha looks over to me.

"She's joking right? There's no way you guys can afford to…" I raise my hands to stop her.

"As far as i'm concerned she can do whatever she wants. She IS the heir to the kingdom afterall. Besides it can't possibly be that much."

Samantha gets a napkin and writes a number down. She passes it to me and I look at it. I stare at it for a moment before handing it back. Looking over to Jade I shrug.

"I thought trade was a way to make a lot of money? My family gets more than that in a month." Samantha stares at me in shock.

"WHAT! Your family makes over a hundred thousand Confederate marks?" Jade interrupts her.

"The Green family currently has sixty-six members of which fifty-two are royal guards, ten more are smiths or enchanter's capable of making the armor the royal guards use. Conner probably has the lowest salary of around forty-thousand a year and that doesn't include prize money of which he's made hundreds of thousands already. Add in the lowest ranking member of the royal guard makes around a hundred thousand a year and the Green's make a lot of money." I nod.

"We also have lands of our own that we administer for the royal family. We get a cut of the taxes there as well. We also don't buy much aside from new weapons and the basic necessities. Since food is provided for most of us we don't buy much of anything now that I think about it." Samantha gaws at me a moment.

"How much have you spent in the last year?" I think for a moment.

"I bought a pistol and ammo plus some gauntlets. So a couple thousand I guess. The rest of my finances just go to my family's funds."

I don't really think of money. The military takes care of my food and provides a place to sleep so no money lost there. I guess I pay taxes but all I need to know is I can afford my custom kit. I don't think the rest of my family does much different.

"Well if your paying I won't question it. Hope you make as much a profit as we will." Jade smiles.

"Oh i'm sure we'll make a profit. The princess that beat the crap out of my guard seems intent on forming a profitable relationship." I grimince.

"I was up against the strongest knights in the world and put two on their ass!" Samantha looks over to me and glances to my side.

"Heard you took quite the injury in that fight. Though it's good to hear you made them work for their victory." I hear murmurs and turn around to see a group of student eavesdropping on us. They split up once they realize we're staring at them but I catch the glaces thrown my way.

"There'll be stories about how your squad killed knights by the end of the night." I look over to Jade who's looking rather smug.

"Great. Cause I always wanted a imperial bounty on my head." Jade's smug smile turns into a frown and even Samantha looks a bit worried.

Imperial bounties were no joke. The Imperium has an impressive number of soldiers of fortune as well as other highly skilled individuals. They take pride in their martial abilities but like Blade they know that a well placed dagger can be more effective than any number of armies.

They used to enjoy their days in the shadows but ever since they rose to be one of only four factions they stopped bothering to hide. Imperial assassins and agents are around every corner, or that's what they say. It's true that at one point in time if you were in a barracks then at least two member were imperial agents. But after a few too many agents were caught and a couple failed assassination attempts they changed tactics.

They made a couple assassinations of high profile people and made it clear that if the Emperor wanted you dead, it was only a matter of time. With a reputation like that not too many people try to become more than a minor nuisance. Of course every now and then somebody does something that demands vengeance. That's where the imperial bounty comes in.

An imperial bounty is like a normal bounty except instead of bounty hunters and thugs coming after you you have highly skilled assassins. Most people with an imperial bounty end up dead inside of a month. The longest person to survive was a pirate named Barbosa. He lived for six years with a bounty on him by staying at sea for as long as possible. Eventually someone collected but his names in the history books now.

If word got around that someone killed an imperial knight it's possible the imperials will put a bounty on me on principle. Then i'll spend my probably short life looking over my shoulder. Though I guess since I kinda do that now anyway. With that thought in my head I turn to glare at the students looking my way. They scatter like ants and I sigh.

"Your a real charmer." I look over to Jade.
"I'm not much interested in being friends with people who piss their parents money away." I feel someone staring at me.

I glance around but noone looking in my direction at the moment. Turning back to the others I still feel a pair of eyes on me. My instincts tell me it's something dangerous. Getting up I excuse myself.

"What's up Conner?" I look over to Samantha.
"Gotta use the little soldier's room." She nods but Jade stares at me for a minute. Ignoring her I head into the crowd of people.

I glance backwards towards the table I left and see two CAs take my place. We'd never leave our charge completely through we'd rather keep our distance. Before I can think more on it I get the feeling of someone watching me again and head to the bathroom.

Entering the bathroom I check to see if anyone's in one of the stalls and am glad to see noone is. I head into one and take off my hat. Picking at a seam inside I take out the hidden blade. It's was little more than a sharpened piece of mettle but it was better than nothing. I hear the door open and a the sounds of feet hitting the floor. Three of them.

Putting on my hat I hide the blade in my left hand and head out of the stall after flushing. I walk up to the sink and look into the mirror to see three men dressed as waiters. They all stare at me and I look at them in the mirror and give a grin.

"Can I help you gentlemen?" They each pull a gun out of their pockets. As soon as I see the guns I shoot backwards into the one in the middle. I hit him in the gut with my elbow and feel the air rush out of his lungs. Before the others react I stab the one to my left with the blade and twist myself around the man I hit.

Six shots ring out but with only a short whissle to let me know they'd be fired. I kick the now very dead man towards the last remaining waiter. He reacts quickly but not quick enough as I punch his face and grab the gun. We wrestle for the gun for a bit until he pulls the trigger in quick succession. Bullets pour out and soon I hear the familiar click of an empty clip.

I let gun of the gun and attempt a punch at his gut but meet his atm. He parries my punch and sends a kick at my left knee. I sidestep to dodge but his attack was a feint. A sharp pain spreads from my gut as his fist lands a solid hit. I gasp for air and get a fist to my face.

I fall backwards and look at the man. He was in a relaxed stance and ready to go another round. I wipe away some blood from my nose and glare at him. I make to charge him but stop when he tenses his muscles to intercept me. Instead of barreling into him I grab one of his comrades guns from their cold dead hands and point it at him. He makes a dash towards the door and I put three rounds into his back.

I grab my blade and head towards the door. Putting the gun in my pocket I open the door and look out. I see two men standing like bouncers in front of the door. Markus and another CA are in front of them staring daggers. When they glance my way the waiters look to me and attempt to bolt. I quickly grab one and pull him inside the bathroom.

When he's inside I begin beating the crap out of him. After several punches to the face I see he's no longer moving. Heading outside I see the parties come to a halt. Looking over to where everyone's stare I see Markus reaching down the waiters throat. I head over and see the clearly dead man.

"Give up Markus he's dead." The other CA who I see is nine shakes his head. "Some sort of suicide pill sir. Tried to stop him." As Markus gives up on stopping the man from taking his own life I shrug.

"It's alright. I got one live one in the bathroom taking a nap." At that nine heads into the bathroom. Some guards come up to Markus and demand his surrender but I step in between them.

"You guys really going to try arresting one of us? After you idiots let assassins aboard?" They look at each other and then pull out cuffs.

"Listen. Until things are sorted out you and your friend here are going to…" I step over to the dead waiter and pull out his gun. I hear several gasps from the students, as I hand it over to the guards.

"Consider things sorted. Now if you require me or my friends to do your job any further you know where to find us." I whistle and see my squad form up around Jade and Samantha. Nine opens the door and shakes his head and I sigh. Must of gone overboard. Damn it.

Chapter 15
The Academy
Conner

12/29/1438

Getting out on deck I see the other students are not the cheerful bunch they were last week. Finding out assassins made it on the boat and were disguised as staff had a way of killing the mood. Thankfully the other islands military intervened quickly to take charge of the ship and replace the staff with their own. For the last week the non-stop parties had been replaced with being locked in rooms with guards.

Several of the other captain's had expressed their thanks to me for stopping the assassins. I shrugged them off with a humble 'Just doing my duty' and went back to guarding Jade. I didn't mean to be rude but ever since the incidents Jade and Samantha have been a bit stir crazy. Thankfully we managed to arrange them in the same room so they have each other to talk to but with half my squad in there at one time they've expressed their feeling of being in prison.

At least now we can get on dry land with a lot better security. Speaking of which reminds me of the icendent. We'd been sailing for several days and the boat had been running all over the Alliance for more than a month before stopping at Blade. These guys were professionals and it shows how good they were by the fact that no one knows when they got aboard. No one knows how, who, or why. The only thing we know is they were probably after me.

If they were after me they had better chances to do it. I spent most of my time away from Jade's side in the library or on deck. I guess the deck has a higher risk of being discovered but the library was fairly isolated. At most there was only a couple people on there and it'd have been easy to gun us all down. So why wait till I was alone in a bathroom to try and kill me?

So many question and no answers. The guy who I thought I'd beaten senseless had actually swallowed a fake tooth filled with poison. The only other clue we have is the pistols used. Twelve round clip, inbuilt silencer, lightweight and compact. Truly masterfully made and something like these would cost a fortune. The easiest answer is that another faction wanted to lynch a couple students but that makes no sense. If that was their plan then they could of gunned down a lot of us in the ballroom.

After a couple minutes of pondering I shrug. This was an investigation that I had no authority over. The only thing I should do is be extra vigilant from now on and make sure Jade is safe. I wish I had gotten to keep that pistol, would've made my job easier.

Looking out I stare at the island we'll be staying at for next couple of years. The island was extra large and from what i've been told it holds around a hundred thousand citizens. They work the lands and tend to the port while those who work at the academy insure a steady supply of tourism in the form of their students. Both get something out of it so everyone is happy.

Besides the towns on the outskirts in the center was the academy. The academy was split into four sections.

Exploration, Scientific, Government, and Military. Each section had the same starting layout. A main building with a dorm adjacent. After that each section was different.

In the Exploration section they have a massive star observation dome. Several smaller observation platforms and even a few balloons cover the area. From their students learn all they need to know to go exploring new lands. Mainly they learn map-making and how to read the stars. They also learn how to identify plants and survive outdoors.

In the Scientific section they have an observation dome and several workshops of various sizes spread all around. This section is home to the best engineers and scientist in the Alliance. Gearbox often remarked that some of the best and the worst idea the Alliance has come up with came from here.

The Government section is a place of sin. Nothing but people talking about politics and the benefits of trade. Luckily i'll only be there for a couple classes, mainly language and one about trade that serves as my turn watching Jade.

Last but best is the military section. Barracks and train yards make up most of the area but what interest me the most is the long flat strip of land that serves as an airstrip. From their the new airplanes are kept and flown by students. My whole squad is taking a lot of lessons here and all of us have the air class. Jade is in it as well so it's work. At least that's what we're going to say in our report.

All in all it was a nice place. We'll be staying in a village where the four sections meet. It's where most of the teachers live as well as some of the students who don't want to live in a dorm. Because of our numbers we'll be split among four houses, making it three per house. Samantha requested to bunk with Jade and we didn't mind. Sam was chosen as the guard that'll stay with them at the house.

Our duty comes first but it'd be irresponsible not to take advantage of this chance to learn new skills. I can only hope me and my squad can take this time to advance ourselves. Hope we don't have to fight off more assassins.

Chapter 16
Tensions Rising

Peace In The South!

1/04/1439

Last month a peace treaty was forged with the Imperium ending hostilities with Alliance personal. Included in the treaty is a promise of free trade in the new lands! With this the Alliance may finally get a leg up over the Confederation in trade. Already a trade fleet from Water's has departed to sell their cargo to Blade. Will this spell the end of the feds strangle hold on trade?

Blade Threatens To Leave The Alliance!

2/12/1439

After several islands complaining over not being allowed to settle on the new lands discovered in the South Blad has stated that they will withdraw from the Alliance before allowing other islands from taking what they've spilled blood for. Verbun and Alleato have stated their agreement with Blade and will join their historic ally if they choose to leave. Many wonder if this is a bluff or if Blade actually intends to leave the Alliance. An emergency council session has been set for next month.

Alliance Stable!

4/21/1439

After a prolonged period of debate all can rest in peace! Blade, Verbun and Alleato have agreed to stay in the Alliance on the condition that they are given sole rights to the new lands. In return they will allow people to immigrate to their colonies. Thousands of families have already signed up to start a new life on new soil.

North Gets Deadly!

2/02/1440

A naval patrol was attacked while attempting to search a suspected pirate vessel. The feds released a statement saying the ship our patrol was investigating was clearly a merchant but no guild has claimed the vessel as theirs. The council has called for more ships to be brought to the North as well as increases to the border islands garrisons.

Trade War?

10/13/1441

The Alliance has declared that until the Imperium declares an end to trade with the Alliance they will not trade with both parties. Insiders stated that the council bursted into laughter when they heard. One council member stated "An empire built on trade can not survive without it."

THE EMPEROR IS DEAD!

12/21/1441

Breaking news from the Imperium! A massive explosion has left the royal palace in ruins. Among the dead is the emperor and his heir. Along with them several members of the imperial elite lost their lives in this attack. Already people are wondering if this will lead to civil war. The Confederation has stated their willingness to aid in any way they can to maintain peace.

Confederation Demands End To Trade War

12/30/1441

The Confederation has sent a letter to our council demanding significant trade concessions as well as a general disarmament. If these demands aren't met then the Confederation say they'll "destroy every ship in the Alliance". The Alliance council has ordered the northern border islands to prepare for potensial invasion.

Aside from that the Council has ordered the central army, fleet, and air force to join up and prepare for a counter attack. The council has also asked for extra donations of money and resources in case of war. Several islands have stated that they'll send financial aid but only five islands have commited military support.

Chapter 17
Reassigned
Conner

1/04/1441

Looking out at all the hands waving goodbye I pick out Samantha and Jade quick enough. It was hard to miss them with the five red plated knights standing around Jade. Seeing Jade waving goodbye besides the rest of my class nearly brings a tear to my eyes.

For the last three years we'd all stayed up late studying for tests. And in that time we also managed more than a couple parties. All in all we'd become surprisingly close and seeing them all here to send us off brings a smile to my lips. When we'd received orders to trade off with the royal guard Jade had tried to countermand the order and had spent several hours on the phone with her father.

Not surprisingly she didn't get our order countered. Blade was sending forces to up North and our company had experience there. HQ isn't about to send our company out with a tenth of it force acting as guards. The only course of action is to recall us and send in the royal guard. They won't be missed if war breaks out and frankly we'd probably die before allowing the rest of our company to leave us behind.

It does suck that we have to leave halfway through but duty calls. Besides everyone got to learn a lot here. Among many academic things we all managed to pick up the imperial tongue as well as learn to fly the UIA's new planes. By far the flying lessons were the most important. It didn't take us long to see that these planes can be easily used as scouts. Add guns and maybe some sort of small bomb and these planes become a new form of direct artillery. I sent all the schematics I could get back to Gearbox and I hope he'll make good use of them.

"Sir!" I turn around to see a couple soldiers in Water's uniform.
"What can I help you with?" I ask hestainly. We were just here as passengers to be transported to Water but there was a gleam in this privates eyes. Just in case I prepare myself for a fight.
"Can we have your autograph?"

What? One of them passes me a pad and a pen and I look at them confused for a moment before realizing their serious. Shrugging I sign my signature and the rest take turns passing me pads of paper. After I sign them all they thank me and head off to their duties. I look around and see a lieutenant standing watch nearby.

I head over to him and ask why some privates would want an autograph. He looks at me and lets out a small chuckle. He explains that everyone in my company is famous on Water. Our squad in particular since we were one of only two that defended the palace. And while no names were released it was known that a male sgt saved their king, so it didn't take long before they figured it was me.
After thanking the man I excuse myself. Heading to my bunk I realize what it was I saw in those privates eyes. It was admiration and respect. Thinking back to the harshness I faced from my own family to be allowed to join the

Combined Arms I can't stop a grin from forming. I'm glad I didn't stay on Blade.

Water
1/11/1441

Looking around I see my peers. All ten sgts from our company were in one room and that made us all uneasy. We'd never been given group briefings. The captain had always given each sgt their squads orders and made sure they understood them. Yet here we all were staring at the grizzled veteran. He looked on all of us as he tapped a map of Water.

"Our entire regiment is here. As you are all no doubt aware our regiment is only at seven companies at the moment but the fact remains we are all here for one purpose. To protect Water." He takes out a pen and circles a port near one of the major rivers leading to the capital.
"This is Whitebridge. It's one of many ports on the beaches of this island and one of the few that is next to a river leading to the capital. It is of vital importance that this port not be taken. To insure it isn't a gate is being constructed out of concrete, that won't be done for another month so until then the four forty mm guns stationed around the port will have to do."

After Jack's raid Water upped its defences. Every outer port had at least two of these massive guns. From what i've heard they'd held off on putting gates in due to financial concerns but with war on the horizon gates are being built all over the rivers. Besides from the new defensive structures i'd heard the army completely reformed. Now numbering around ninety thousand soldiers they have little trouble garrisoning their ports properly. That said the bulk of their military force is still conscripts and militia.

"The fifth company has been given the honor of defending this location. It is believed to be the most likely to be attacked in case of invasion due to its river connecting not just to the capital but also to several other major cities. Its dockyard is also one of the largest in the Alliance and would be a boon to any military endevor in the area. It's tactical and strategic importance can't be understated."

If war came then Water would be on the frontline. It's dockyards would be a great asset to our fleets as a repair and refueling station. Likewise it'd also be a great place for the Confederation to use as a base of operations against the Alliance. If we lost Water we'd be limited on how far our navies can go, and we could forget about any offensive operations.

"Of course we won't be doing this job alone. Ten thousand soldiers from Water's army are here and another five from the Alliance central army. It's still a large town and our anti ship capabilities are low, so don't let the large numbers fool you." He points to an apartment block about ten miles out from the dockyard.

"First and second squads will be stationed here. The area is mostly apartments for the dockworkers and a small park. Should be plenty of places to set up ambushes and stall the enemy. And that sums up your job nicely. Until the feds commit you'll hold the line here with platoon to support you. Once the feds have sent in the main force ours will begin a counter attack to drive them into the sea."

He goes over the other squads orders but I focus on the area i'll be defending. Residential areas are hard to take and easy to defend if you know what your doing. No matter what through the fighting will be hard of course. It'll likely devolve into fighting building to building until one side is dead. Of course as the defending side i'll be able to set up traps as well as have machine gun emplacements ready. But only two squads and a platoon limits my options.

Water's standard platoon was forty men in four squads lead by a second lieutenant and a senior sergeant. That means we'll have sixty soldiers to defend the area. I'll need to requisition some things but a plan was forming in my head. For their sakes I hope the feds don't come here.

Chapter 18
War
Conner

1/23/1441

Looking at the sandbags being placed between the streets and in the alleys I can't help but think of all the people that would normally be walking around. Once war was declared last week the citizens were asked to vacate the city to be out of the way. Almost all of them joined the army or militia. The only ones who didn't being the ones unable to fight due to age or injury.

"Sgt Green!" I look over and see a man dressed in a dark grey uniform. He was lieutenant Wilhelm, the leader of the platoon here. Since the water's army reformed they switched to a dark grey uniform like the Alliance central forces.

"As I said before LT Wilhelm I go by Alpha one during operations." He nods. He's a young officer. One of the many that joined after Jack's raid.
"Of course sir! Sorry sir!" I look the young man up and down. Sixteen, maybe eighteen years old. I guess I can't judge. I'm only twenty-three myself and if I learned one thing at the academy it's that I should be more social with my peers. Even if they seem too young.
"Relax LT. We may be at war but last sighting of the feds says their attacking other islands first. No point in being tense now." He takes a moment to take a breath. After a couple seconds he speaks again.

"Sir. I was wondering where you were planning on placing your squad."

At the moment we only have ten men stationed on the street. As for the rest of Wilhelms platoon, they were stationed in buildings behind the defensive line with three machine guns. They'd be giving supporting fire from above and should the main line be overwhelmed, they'll make great reinforcements.

As for my men I have options. Putting them in the buildings gives them superior cover but will leave the line weak. Putting them on the line risks losing all of them to a grenade or artillery fire if the feds manage to set it up. Spitting them up is the best option.

"I'll have five of us on the line and the rest can keep you company." Wilhelm nods again. I feel like i'm giving orders to a puppy. Hopefully after he gets some experience he'll be able stand on his own legs. "Also the men are wondering if they should be addressing you as captain or…"
"Alpha one or just A one is fine." I interrupt him.

The problem with working with other units is that their ranks are different. CA's have private, sergeant, captain, major, then general. So when we work with other islands platoons, something which we don't even have, it can be hard to judge who's in command. LT Wilhelm is on paper senior to me, but if we take into account our different branches then i'm very much his senior.

I'm lucky when I think about it. Wilhelm is ok with taking orders from me. I heard some of the other regiments are having are a hard time integrating with local forces. As i'm thinking of how lucky I am a soldier comes running up to us.

Snapping a quick salute he addresses us both.

"Confederate ships spotted by patrol. Large formation. Two days out." Wilhelm looks a bit worried but shrugs it off after glances my way.
"Did our navy engage?" The runner shakes his head.
"From what i've been told our fleet broke off after confirming the enemy's strength." Wilhelm looks grim but I place a hand on his shoulder.
"Good! Wouldn't want the navy to have all the fun would we lieutenant?" He looks my way then his face breaks into a smile.
"That's true. If the feds come here we'll show them the fruits of our training!" His platoon who'd been watching let out a cheer. Backing off I watch them go back to preparing defences with smiles and grins.

Watching all of them cheerily preparing for the battle to come I can't help but feel proud to be serving alongside them. They may not be up to Blade's standards of training but no one can doubt their commitment. They'll fight to the last man defending their homes. I just hope that they have no need to.

1/26/1441

The loud booms from the dockyard guns can be hear clearly. Looking beside me I can see the soldier's tense. The four CA's also tense but there's is different. Like me they can't wait for this. We were bred for war and now it was coming to us. Deep inside we all were thankful for this chance to prove ourselves on the field of battle.

After what seems an eternity of waiting I see a soldier in a window motion down the street. They were here. A couple shots rip into the sandbags but none of us move. After several more shots are fired into our wall the streets would be quite if not for the sound of the dock's guns letting us know they had not fallen. I hear the sounds of feet approaching us but make no sound. All the soldier's on the line hold their breath with me.

A whistle barks out and I rise enough to lift my rifle over the waist high wall. I see a full platoon of men and woman in bright red uniforms all looking shocked with surprise. I open fire along with the others on the line and as I do the roar of machine gun fire deafens me.

In seconds the platoon is dead. Their bodies ripped to bloody shreds from our attack. The street was running with their blood. None of us care about that though as the sounds of boots can be heard. We all prepare to fire and as the first spot of red moves into view we all open fire. After a minute nothing moves and we stop.

Then a canister is thrown into the street. White smoke begins to fill the street and I can hear the sound of wood and glass being broken. They were using the smokescreen to buy time to move into the buildings. I fire into the fog but have no way of knowing if my shots connect. The others follow soon but the machine guns don't waste their valuable ammo on unseen foes.

After the last bullet leaves my rifle I kneel down and eject the spent clip. Reaching for aa full one i'm nearly knocked backwards as a loud bang rips through the street. Loading a new clip in I return to a firing position to see a small crater where an enemy grenade must of gone off. It was close to our line but not close enough to be a concern just yet.

As I think that the man next to me lets out a howl of pain and falls back. Turning to him I see him cradling his shoulder. Setting my rifle aside I take out my knife and cut off his sleeve to see the wound clearly. I check for an exit wound and to my relive I find it. Using the sleeve i'd just cut off him I bandage him up.

"Lucky for you it went clean through. Fall back and get a real bandage on you and you'll be fine." He looks like he's about to say something but just then the machine guns open up and drown out his words.

Turning away from him I see the smokescreen has begun to clear up. It was not hard to see all the Confederate soldier's in the windows and doorways. I hug the sandbags for cover as the feds begin pouring fire at us. A woman cries out as she's hit and turning to look I see she's taken one to the side of the head.

One of mine begins tending to her but as he does and shot takes him in the shoulder and falls down. Laying down a bullet whizzes by where my head was a moment ago. Looking back I see our machine gunners unleashing a hail of iron down on the feds.

I raise my rifle and fire blindly. To try and raise my head above the sandbags would be suicide now. Another bang goes off and I feel the force of a small explosion. Another grenade, this one closer. They were advancing, slowly but surely. I take out a smoke and drop it over it the sandbag. Another one follows and then another. Before long the street is once again filled with dense smoke.

I take the time to order some men to take the wounded away. With them gone the line was down to ten including me. Gesturing to the others I lead them away from the sandbags and back towards the building with our comrades. We quickly disperse to doorways and alleys to take cover.

When the smoke clears the shooting resumes but now I could see soldier's piling up at our old defensive line. They were cowering before our machine guns and I couldn't blame them. I take aim and fire at a man and am rewarded with a spray of blood spurting from his chest. Two more follow their friend before i'm forced to shrink back into the building.

I hear a loud bang as a boot hits wood. Heading inside i'm blindsided as a man tackles me. Taking out my knife I stab the man in his side. As his grip loosens I drop the knife in favor of his sidearm. Taking his pistol out of his holster I fire in the direction he had come.

Another man falls back as three bullets tear into him but I can see another hiding. They had come in from the back from a side alley. The one major problem with city fighting is you never know where the enemy will kill you. Pushing the dead man off me I toss a grenade through the door. Several voices cry out in pain as the grenade goes off. I can only imagine the shrapnel cutting into men who were probably about to charge in.

I head over to the back to see if any more are coming. Peeking out I almost lose my head as a saber buries itself in the door frame. Leaping back I see a officer charging towards me with their sword raised. I use the pistol to parry the blade the punch th man in the gut. I then give him a sharp whack on the head with the butt of the pistol and he goes down like a rock. Before I can check to see if he's dead screams and shouts draw my attention away.

Heading back to the street I see the feds have decided to attempt a breakthrough. Their corpses now litter the street. This whole street was a kill box and I can only hope the officer who ordered their men to charge into it died with them. Attempting to evaluate my position I see another CA looking towards me. He waves for me to come over and after a brief moment of hesitation I run across the street. A couple shots belt the ground around me but I manage to get to other side without getting shot.

Up close I recognize alpha two and put a hand on his shoulder.
"Good to see your still kicking." He nods and turns to point up the stairs.
"Orders came through. Counter attack is beginning and we should see friendly forces in the next couple minutes." I open my mouth but am interrupted as he grabs me and throws me to the side.

I crash into the wall and look up to see him wrestling with a fed. Pulling out my pistol I aim for the man's back when another comes in. I quickly change targets and shoot him in the arm. He charges towards me and i'm forced to put two more rounds into him before he slumps to the floor. By the time he falls alpha two has disarmed and impaled his opponent with his own rifle.

Getting up I reload my pistol in time to meet another bach of feds charging in. Two of them come at and another three head towards alpha two. I kill the ones heading toward me long before they can engage with their bayonets. I also deprive my friend of his fun by killing his assailants as well. After that a couple soldiers come down from the stairs with rifles raised.

They see us standing over the bodies of our enemies and promptly return to their positions upstairs. I reload my pistol again and Alpha two takes out his own. After a second I holster my pistol and grab one of the fed's rifles. Checking to make sure there's a bullet in the chamber I prepare to meet another charge.

I don't have to wait long before another bach of soldiers attempt to storm us. Most of them die before they realize where we are and the few who survive are killed by either my bayonet or alpha two's knife.

Seeing a grenade fly through the door I ditch the rifle i'd embedded into a soldier. Diving for the grenade I just manage to catch it. Not wasting time I toss it back without a second thought. A heartbeat later the grenade goes off and shrieks of pain tell me they had grouped at the door.

Drawing my sword in my right hand I take out my pistol with my left. I look over to alpha two and give him a smile before I run through the door.

Getting back on the street I see the remains of the enemy all around. Between the grenade and our friends upstairs the feds have lost a large number of soldiers. While seeing how effective our defence reassures me I can't help but gawk at the still breathing confederate soldiers. For every dead one there seems to be another two running for cover.

I make my way to another building across the street and spot a squad preparing to breach a apartment. One was holding the door open while his friend was priming a grenade. I wait till I see the door start to push open and the man starts to toss the grenade before I fire. A bullet hits the man in the arm and this forces him to drop the grenade.

At best they have a couple seconds to react. This squad uses those precious seconds to form up and prepare to return fire. I could see in their eyes that they hadn't even thought about their actions. They had simply done what they'd been trained to do. I felt a pain of pity for them as the grenade went off. Not their fault if they had faulty training.

Any pity is removed from my mind when a bullets start pelting the ground and wall around me. I open the to peek in and see a rifle pointed my way. Instead of blowing my head off it's bearer smiles and welcomes me in like we're old friends meeting for a meal. Inside was a bakery, it's tables that not so long ago probably had cherry customers were now being used as operating tables. Wounded soldiers were stretched out and being treated by a single medic who looked ready to collapse.

I nod to the soldier guarding the door and enter. Closing the door behind me I take a minute to exam the improvised hospital. Three men and a woman were on tables. One of them I see is the man who i'd sent way earlier and another I recognize as bravo seven. I head over to him and a deep sense of despair washes over me. He's been shot twice in the chest and taken another to the shoulder. I put a hand on his neck and find a weak pulse.

He's lost a lot of blood. Looking at his bandages I can see he was in the best state possible. His fate was now beyond any medic's power. Turning away from him I look at the other wounded. Before I do a I hear a shot ring out and turn to see the door open and a fed falling back.

Instantly my weapons are raised and i'm heading towards the door. Three soldiers enter in an attempt to overwhelm the guard but they're met with my charge. I slash my sword across the first one's chest. Before he hits the ground I kick another so hard he falls back outside the door. The other makes to stab me with his bayonet but before he can skewer me he falls clutching at his neck.

I salute the soldier and then head out the door. I meet a woman who was about to peek into the door. Her head is cut in half from my sword. Two others are helping the man i'd kicked out up and attempt to react to me. I shoot all three of them in rapid succession. Looking around I see more and more feds clogging the street. Many of the buildings now had blown out windows or were riddled with bullet holes.

Hearing movement behind me I turn and raise my pistol. A smile grows on my face when I see several soldiers in

Alliance uniforms charging down the street. I take cover as they begin to pour fire into the enemy ranks. Volley after volley is fired down the street until nothing moves. Those who managed to find cover in doorways and alleys returned fire but it was poorly aimed and lacked any semblance of discipline. They were no longer fighting to advance, no now they fought just to survive.

We don't let up. I take whoever is able and join our comrades in the counter attack. As one we march through the streets. Every now and again we find a squad or two but they are quickly overwhelmed by our firepower. I soon find that my pistol is hardly needed. The soldiers of the Alliance worked as one to make sure not a single enemy is left standing. In no time at all we're at the dockyard. Here the feds make their stand.

Crates, carts, doors, all were used to make a barricade that confederate soldiers were hoping to stop our counter attack. Unlike the rest of this battle the feds now had the advantage. The only way was forward and that way had hundreds of rifles behind cover to meet us. If they had a single machine gun then any hope of storming them is merely a dream. As is the shear number of rifles would make a charge near impossible to complete.

An order comes down for us to wait and so we do. Just out of range of the feds we begin building our own defences. Tearing off doors, finding tables and bookcases, we take everything we can to fortify our position. After we finish we stared at the feds opposite us. After a while feds trickle through other streets followed by more Alliance soldiers. By the time the sun begins to set we had thousands ready to charge in.

Mortars are brought up and carefully aimed to avoid collateral damage. The docks are of vital importance and blowing them up is almost as bad as allowing the enemy to take them. Hours go by before the mortars are ready to fire. After so much waiting and staring at the enemy, it's time to shove them into the sea.

With the moon illuminating our battlefield the mortars open fire. All along the enemy lines their barricades are blown to bits. More than a few feds get blow away along with their cover. As the final mortar goes silent a roar goes out from our ranks. With a whistle our commanders let us off our leashes and we charge howling and screaming like mad men at our opponents.

I find myself at the front of my section of the charge. Bullets whizz by me and I feel the adrenaline pumping through my tired body. Getting to the enemy line I jump over a crater and start stabbing feds with my sword. Like a scythe before wheat I cut down the enemy along with my fellow soldiers. Anyone who puts up a fight is met with three more of us to bring them down quickly.

After a day of fighting it all ends with this charge. We drive them to their boats and then harass them until their out of our range. When the last transport is out of sight a cheer goes through our ranks. This city shall remain free to fight the feds another day.

Chapter 19
Battle For Water
Conner

2/06/1441

Staring through the scope I make out confederate soldiers digging a new trench lines. If the reports were right then nearly ten thousand feds were over there preparing a landing zone for their forces. After failing to take a port capable of handling their numbers they have decided to simply make one somewhere else. By the time we realized what they were doing they'd already dug too deep for us to drag them out.

Now they were expanding their trenches to accommodate their growing numbers. Taking aim at one of the laboring soldiers I shoot him in the chest and he falls back. His friends all drop their tools and dive for cover while the man next to marks another slash on a piece of paper.

"Another confirmed kill for alpha one." Alpha two was smirking at the kill sheet. Over a hundred marks were in the paper. "Alpha three and ten will be sad once they realize you've passed them again." I grin as I shoot another fed in the head.
"They'll pass me by the days end. How's four and seven?" I finish my sentence with another pull of the trigger. Far in the distance a fed who'd tried to make a break for it falls over dead.
"Their stable but won't be released for another couple days. We got off lucky." I sigh in agreement.

We'd only had wounded. Bravo squad had lost two members killed. Some of if not the first CA casualties in this war. Hopefully the last as well. I recall seeing bravo two's face. We don't use our names while on mission for this reason. Our mission must come before mourning and bravo two has shown her ability to do just that. She didn't even flinch when she got the news nor did she hesitate to volunteer for the next mission.

As a fellow officer in the same branch I can relate with her. It's one thing to mourn a friend or comrade, it's another to constantly wonder if your orders or actions got them killed. The guilt, real or imaginary, eats at you. Just hearing that some of my squad had been wounded was enough to ruin any sense of victory. I'm sure one day i'll look back and see this as a victory but for now I have a bitter taste about the whole thing. I wonder how the higher ups can stomach it all.

Thinking about my comrades deaths I can at the very least say we died for a noble cause. What will they tell the parents of the children i'm killing? Who has their deaths served? I see no other reason for them to be here other than to exhaust our bullets.

"We got movement." I adjust my scope so that I can get a wider view. From our position on a hill just behind our trench line I could see our own forces getting into positions. Looking towards the enemy lines I see a giant white mist coming our way. A smokescreen.
Artillery opens up in an attempt to get a lucky hit in but our infantry holds fire. The mist continues to get closer and when it's only a couple hundred yards away the whole line opens fire. Thousands of men work together to make a wall of

bullets to kill any would be attackers.

Eventually the mist stops uncomfortably close to our lines. Our fire has stopped now. We can't use up all our ammo in a single day now can we? As i'm thinking that I hear the cry of mortars firing through the air. Explosions rip through our lines and a whole section of the trench is reduced to craters.

The feds begin pouring through the mist and charge towards the gap in our line. I hear alpha two grab their rifle and we both open fire on them. We aren't the only ones. To either side of them the unaffected trench sections opened fire on them. Unfortunately the feds choose their target well and have significantly weakened the amount of fire we can throw at their assault.

While our riflemen are able to pour fire into them our machine guns overlapping fire has been broken. Now only a few guns are in a position to fire at the assault. Even with the other sniper teams acting as support it was clear that the feds were going to reach the gap with plenty of manpower to force a breakthrough. If something isn't done then we'll be forced to withdraw and the feds will have their landing zone.

Just then a bright flare shoots up in the air and begins to arc towards the gap. It's blue and gold color was a signal for all CAs to gather. Icould see the other sniper teams leaving their positions to head over to the defences and for a brief moment I see captain steel. I'm on my feet in an instant and alpha two is right behind me.

Charging towards the gap i'm joined by the rest of my squad and off to ethir side I see the other squads of my company. I couldn't help smiling as I recall that not so long ago we were all in the same class. Now we would all fight in the same mud.

Getting to the rows of craters that make up the gap in our lines I slide down one. Me and my squad set up and begin firing our rifles into the oncoming enemies. Fire, pull back bolt, aim, fire. For several minutes that's all any of us do. Then the feds start throwing themselves into the craters we are using as cover.

I find myself face to face with an ugly man with burns covering half his face. He attempts to stab me with his bayonet but I swipe it away with my own rifle and shoot him point blank in the chest. Quickly I pull back the bolt and fire at another man who was preparing to shoot another of my men.

A woman swings a sword at me and I block it with the barrel of my rifle. The steel of her sword buries itself in the wood of my rifle until it gets stuck on the metal barrel. I push up and let go of my rifle. This staggers her and before she can recover my sword has cut open her stomach and she falls. I try to see how the rest of my squad is doing but two more feds throw themselves at me.

I parry one's rifle but the other gets a glancing blow on my left arm. I kick his friend away them seperate his head from the rest of him. Turning back to the other I just barely parry a thrust that would of seen to the end of me. A quick thrust of my sword makes short work of him. After killing the last of my current assailants I draw my pistol and scan my squads status.

Everyone is fighting their own attacker and some had the

misfortune to be fighting two or even three at once. I'm about to help one of my outnumbered comrades when I see a couple feds getting read to fire into our crater. Three shots head their way and three feds fall dead before they let off a single shot. I'm feeling pretty good about things until a hulking arm grabs me by the arm and throws me out of the crater.

I land on top of a now very confused confederate soldier. Getting up I make sure to stab him. I'm forced to use the rest of my pistols clip to get some breathing room. After I manage that I jump back in the crater and see the man who tossed me out like garbage.

Of course the feds have a giant. Six feet tall and with muscles straining against their uniform. He was about to smash alpha five so I charge towards him. Before I get to him he turns and smiles as I run my sword through his gut. He continues to smile as he grabs my hand and begins crushing it. I fall to a knee from the pain and drop my pistol. Thinking quickly I take out Gear's gun and shoot the man in the chest. The now familery roar rips out and I smile as I see the dinner plate hole in the giants chest. Even a giant can't fight with a...shit.

Through luck or the last efforts of a dying man he falls on me. I try to dodge out of the way but his grip on my hand is like iron. I have a brief moment to contemplate my life before i'm pinned under the dead man's massive frame. I struggle to get air in my now starving lungs until finally they are allowed a reprieve. With air running through my lungs I go to get myself free but realize the impossibility of the task. I'd need to release his death grip which would require turning him completely over.

Before I can attempt this backbreaking feat I see a woman going to stab alpha three in the back. Thinking quickly I take one of the bullets out of my gauntlet with my teeth and put it in. It only takes a second for me to reload but it feels like hours while I watch the woman get closer to killing my subordinate. Finally I fire and the bullet misses the mark i'd placed on her chest. Instead her arm is completely blown off from the blast and leaves her screaming on the ground.

As much as i'm sure that'll haunt me later I can't think about it now. I reload and fire at another man who was about to open up my skull with their bayonet. He flies back as his chest is broken open. At least his death was quick I think as I reload. I take the little time i've got to try and lift the dead giant off me. I move him a good couple inches before he falls back on me.

I only have seconds before more feds come pouring in and my squad is busy fighting for their lives. Without much thought I place the gun on the man's side and pull the trigger. The bullet tears through what was left of his chest and I am rewarded with now being able to get up. Unfortunately his hand is still stopping me. Holstering my gun I take out a knife and start cutting the man's fingers away. The task is as long as it is disgusting.

Finally i'm free just in time for a confederate soldier to slice the back of my leg and force me to a knee. I turn and parry him with my now free sword. He finds my blade buried in his chest half a second later and falls back. Getting up I nearly trip over all the corpses now littering the crater. A bullet whizzes by my head and I duck down.

A woman makes to enter the crater but a bullet takes her in

the side and she falls to the side instead. I mentally thank whoever did that then begin looking for my pistol. It takes me a minute due to being interrupted every couple seconds but eventually I find my pistol. I begin reloading only to be stopped by a confederate sgt. She demonstrates great skill with a blade and before I know what's going on she has disarmed me. Both my pistol and sword leave me under her assault. Without a weapon i'm forced to do some reckless attacks. I try to grab her sword arm but just get a slice across the arm for my trouble. This wasn't going to end well. She makes a thrust at me but her foot gets stuck on one of her fallen comrades. Finally some good luck!

She's left open for a second and i'm able to tackle her to the ground and stop her from stabbing me. That done I attempt to beat the crap out of her but am stopped when she claws at my eyes. I instinctively fall back and she uses this chance to shove me off of her. Rolling back I come to a stop with gear's pistol pointed at her chest. Her eyes open in shock then acceptice. I pull the trigger and she falls back in a spray of gore.

For a moment I truly do feel disgusted with myself. She was an expert with her blade and killing her this way just felt wrong. My feeling of pity are ended when a confederate bullet rips through my shoulder. I fall back and see alpha three shoot the bastard but I fall back behind my men as they form a line in front of me. Alpha five goes to bandage my shoulder but before he does a bullet hits him in the chest. He falls back and I scramble on top of him.

He's gasping for air while I search for his wound. Instead of finding a wound I find a dented piece of metal. I smile at him.

"Your one lucky son of a bitch!" He nods as he takes in breath then I go silent as I hear the long whistle of artillery.

I cover five in a embrace that I hope protects him. Then several blasts of hot air and a rumbling ground alert me to the shells hitting their marks. I felt a unseen force driving me into the ground and five yelped in pain. As fast as it had come it went away and I got up to survey the field.

It wasn't the feds who had fired. The area where they had been charging from now had several craters far larger than the ones we had been fighting in. The enemy have been soundly beaten. Their assaulting force now lay in literal tatters. Another whine pierced the air but this time none of us ducked for cover. We were far too stunned at the scene in front of us.

Silently we watch as the assaulting force is ripped to shreds by artillery. Whole platoons simply vanish, only to be replace with a crater. It was a horrifying scene but we all were grateful for it. This meant the battle was over, at least for now. We can take time to lick our wounds and remake our defences. That was something we can all smile about.

2/21/1441

I slump to the ground in exhaustion. Looking around at the rest of my squad I see most them do the same. We've been sent to every gap or breakthrough in our defensive line since the feds first breakout attempt. It's the same everyday. The Confederate artillery weakens a certain section of the line, then a smoke screen comes to give their troops some cover. Before they can get through we get there and hold the line long enough for ether artillery or infantry support to reach us.

Every time we do this fewer of us return to camp. Last I checked we'd lost nineteen. To our allies that would be seen as a victory in itself, but to us it's getting far too high. Our company was a hundred strong when we arrived to Water. Losing almost twenty percent of our forces was heartbreaking to us. Even if we take out the emotions of it we still have the cold facts.

It takes fourteen years for a parent to raise their child to the age where they can enlist. If they choose the Combined Arms it'll take another year to finish training. Assuming they pass at such a young age, which only three have managed, then it takes fifteen years to replenish loses. Of course this is discarding the fact that we have plenty of people in CA training, but even then its a year before reinforcements can be given and then at most only around a thousand. If we're being honest the best we can hope for is around a hundred.

It doesn't take a math genius to figure out that with numbers like those the regiments are going to start losing combat effectiveness quickly. There's always the option of combining regiments but that raises a lot of problems. For starters every company specializes in their own thing and even if their in the same regiment they'd have completely different ideas about how to operate.

Hell when I think about it our training really dropped the ball when it came to company or regiment tactics. Guess I shouldn't be surprised. Just last month i'd have said a single company would be able to hold Water without fail. Now I wish our regiment had been finished before the war broke out.

A horn blares through the camp and all of us groan. It's a call to battle, and we must answer. Dragging myself up I grab a rifle and fix the bayonet. Looking at the others I start to say something to raise their spirits but the only thing that comes out is a yawn. Smiles break out on their faces and a coupe even manage a tired laugh. I smile myself, and together we head out to the battle with high moral.

2/22/1441

How the hell did we manage this? Shaking my head I clear my mind of such useless thoughts. We can all have a meeting about our current tactical disaster after we live through it. Thinking that I duck down as bullets belt the area my head had been.

Looking to the other members of my squad I shrug. "Yup they're still there." Half hearted smiles greet my attempt at a joke.
"I've got to give it to the feds. They really managed to out due themselves here." I nod as mortar shells start raining on our improvised trench circle.

Yesterday we had come to plug a hole the feds had made and meet their charge only to get pinned down by artillery. We adapted as quickly as we could and had started digging a trench line when we saw the rest of our line withdrawing. The feds had made a feint and attacked another section of the line with their infantry while leaving their artillery to make sure we couldn't rush to their aid. Most soldiers would think the best course of action would be to make a break for it. Those soldiers would probably be dead.

If we'd attempted a retreat the artillery would of shredded us to bits. The best course of action was to prepare for when they encircle us and hope for reinforcements. A hope that wasn't really shared among anyone here. We had dug our trench circle and even laughed as the feds dug defences around us. I'm sure they would of prefered to blow us to pieces but their big guns were needed to hold the gains they'd made.

Our luck huh? No one around me was complaining. In fact since we saw the feds begin digging in an unnatural calm had settled over the company. We all knew we were probably going to die here and that moment there is nothing to fear! If we know we're about to die then what's the point of worrying about it? The best thing we can do is keep calm and try to make the enemy earn their prize.

I recall drill sergeants hammering those words into us. We were all calm because this is what our instructor had drilled into our young minds. The harder the fight, the calmer we became. The calmer we were, the sharper our teeth. Something we all planed to show the feds before we died.

A whistle breaks through my thoughts and I glance over the top to see the red uniforms of confederate soldiers charging towards us. Locating the source of the noise I raise my rifle. One second later the whistle stops as the officer holding it fell back into their own trench. Then I started firing as fast as I could. Ten aimed shots in under a minute. That's the best we can do before being forced to reload. Together my squad is able to fire a hundred rounds a minute and even through our company is spread in a circle so we can't make the best of our numbers that's still around a thousand shots every minute.

Under such fire the wave of enemy troops breaks after only three minutes. They had made it halfway to our positions before they fell back to their own lines. It was a great sight, seeing a numerically superior enemy running for cover. Hundreds of dead soldiers lay between our lines now. Cheers ran through the company. We would hold till relieved, or until we died.

2/25/1441

I'm out of ammo? Searching my pockets I kneel down to take off of my pack. Raffling through my pack I find no more ammo for my rifle. Putting my pack back on I raise my rifle and pretend to fire. It wasn't long before I noticed others doing the same. We were running dry.

Thankfully the feds choose this time to withdraw. They'll learn we're out of ammo on their next attack. Laying a hand on my grenades I smile as I picture soldiers at ease when they realize their enemy had lost their bite. They'll learn the hard way that we still have a lot of bite left.

2/28/1441

With pistols raised we all fired six shots a minute. Our range had been reduced as well as the amount of enemy troops we could kill before they reached effective range. Out of rifle ammo we were forced to expend our sidearms limited ammo. It was unfortunate. We prefered to use our pistols when we got into melee to help control the area and keep the enemy from overwhelming us. It also meant we had to let the feds get close.

I saw out of the corner of my eye a CA go down as a bullet took them in the neck. I go over to him and clamp my hands over their neck. I see his eyes opening wide from shock and feel his body thrashing around. He is dying. Taking a hand away from his throat I grab a bandage from my back pocket and begin tying it around his neck. After a moment I hear explosions go off and know that many of my comrades are expanding their grenades.

The man i'm bandaging up has stopped convulsing. Now his eyes had taken a calm glassed over look. He smiled and held out his hand. I knew this man. We'd eaten in the mess together during training, we'd fought beside each other several times throughout the month. And now he breathed his last breath and died in my arms. Closing his eyes I set him up against the dirt wall. His last smile made it seem as if he only sleeping but I knew he was well and truly dead.

Reloading my pistol I stand up and prepare to avenge my fallen comrade. Six soldiers fall as I fire as fast as I can aim. Their deaths due little to quell the rising bloodlust in my heart though. A small part of me wanted them to get into melee so that I may cut them down. The urge is quickly abandoned as a wash of shame threatens to overwhelm me.

Reloading my pistol with the last of my ammo I fire again and this time I don't feel a thing. I'm back to my training, simply firing at a enemy that might as well not be human. If I let emotion get involved then i'd be useless in this fight. I can feel emotion after I die.

3/11/1441

Stabbing the man through their chest i'm forced to disregard my rifle in favor of my sword as a woman attempted to run her bayonet through my side. As my blade extends I use it to parry my opponents rifle and then use my other hand to punch her in the gut. She drops her rifle and then I cut her chest open in a quick slash of my sword. Before I can get my bearings back a great weight forces me to the ground.

Turning around I see the flash of steel and prepare to meet my ancestors but instead my assailant is knocked aside by another CA. They begin fighting and another confederate soldier jumps into the fray. Drawing Gear's pistol I watch as the man is blown back as so many before him. At this point i've grown used to people being blown apart. I reload and get up.

I use the gun Gearbox had given me a lifetime ago to great effectiveness. Yet all too quickly I run out of ammo and for the first time in my life i'm completely out of ammo. I think about the power of Gear's creation and in one fluid motion destroy it with my sword. The only one to use this weapon would be me.

As I think that a sword pierces my side. I fall to the ground from a combination of pain and exhaustion. The blade is taken out of my side and I turn to see my opponent. I try to raise my sword but I am far too slow. Before he can finish me off a bequal goes off in the distance and distracts him for a fraction of a second. This costs him his life when my sword pierces his heart.

I see the remaining confederate soldiers leave the trench. They leave behind several of their friends who now lay with many of our own. Five comes over to bandage me and while he does so I see the rest searching the dead for supplies. With the number of dead here we should be able to fully resupply our forces. Though it helps that we probably don't have many people to supply anymore.

3/16/1441

Another push by the feds is now laying dead or retreating back to their trench. With a groan I fall back and slide against wall. Several others do the same but we all know our break will be short lived. Running a hand through my hair I wonder whatever became of my hat. I let a smile form on my lips when I think about what my instructors would say.
"You call yourself an officer? You should be laughing at the enemies attempts to attack you! Hell you should show them pity for their mistake."

I wonder what they'd think of me sitting on my ass in a glorified ditch. They'd probably wonder why i'm so tired. With the food the feds so kindly delivered to us we should be able to repel assault after assault without fail. Even with the heavy loses we'd sustained they'd expect us to fight with the same vigor we had at full strength.

Five comes over to me and examines my wound. His face looks grim and I look down to see my wound had clearly become infected. The skin was a sickly yellow and leaked not blood but a clear puss. Five looked at me and I could tell there was little he can do.

He calls over six and together they start a small fire. Five places a knife over the fire and six hands me a belt to bite on. Mentally preparing myself I wait for the pain to come. When it does it is so intense I think he's stabbing me. Perhaps he was if he thought the infection was deep enough to warrant it. Digging my teeth into the leather belt I manage to hold back the scream building in my throat. This was a pain i'd not wish on my worst enemy.

After what feels like hours five finally takes away the knife and six begins cleaning my wound with what little water we have left. I stop him before he can waste such a valuable resource. He glares at me a moment before six takes the bottle.

"If you get infected you'll die." I glare at him. The pain I felt at his hands did little to improve my mood even if it was to save my life.

"If I die, I die. If we run out of water we all die." Six and five both growl their displeasure. Before they can continue arguing with me another voice interrupts them.

"Alpha one?" I look up and see a slightly familiar face. One of the aids captain Steel had with him to run messages to other units.

"Juliett ten right? What can I do for you?" He glances at my wound with fresh burn marks before giving his report.

"Captain Steel has been rendered unable to command the company. Your next in line sir." The mood dims and I imagine that the grim looks on five and six faces mirrored my own.

"What are our standing forces?" The rest of my squad stops pretending not to be listening in to hear this question. We all knew that we'd taken loses but none of could even guess at how many had died.

"We've lost fifty-seven. Forty-eight of which have died." If the mood was grim before then it has become overwhelmingly depressing now.

Seventy-six percent casualties. Only twenty-four soldiers fit for battle. The nine wounded were also a problem. If they were listed as unable to fight then that meant they were unable to move their arms. If you could move an arm then you can fight.

"Orders sir?" I almost laughed. What order could I give? We had less than three squads to fight the feds back. The only thing we could do was die with honor. From the amount of dead around us I can safely say that we can all meet our ancestors with pride.

"Spread the word. We shall feast on what food we have gotten from the feds and meet our end with such valor that the enemy shall remember us in their nightmares for the next thousand years!" Smiles break out and a cheer begins to spread among us. So what if we died? Our deeds shall be engraved in legend!

3/28/1441

A white flag was being raised in the distance. They wanted to parly. With some reluctance I ordered a white flag raised to match theirs. After a few moments a confederate soldier came out of their trench and I went out to meet him halfway. Both of us could be killed in an instant but none of us even doubted our soldiers. Breaking a flag a truce was considered dishonorable even by pirates. It was often the only thing that would save lives.

Meeting the man it becomes clear that he's a major. His uniform was spotless while mine was covered in mud and several holes made it look like i'd been shot numerous times. His jet black hair was flowing in the wind while my own was cut jaggedly. He salutes me and returning his respect I do the same.

"You've been a real pain." I smile. Weather the man meant that as a compliment I didn't care.

"We have a reputation to uphold." I'm sure that i'm supposed to say something good about his men's actions but all I can see is men and woman that have died for no good reason.

"I'll get to the point. I request your units surrender. I promise you'll be treated fairly under the articles of war." I shrugg.

"I'm sorry but my language doesn't know the meaning of the word." Up until now we'd been speaking in his tongue but now I spoke in my own. To my surprise he responds in it.

"Yes I know about Blade's opinion on warfare. You'll fight until the end because it just might mean the difference between victory of defeat." I shrug.

"We like to think of it as a good death." He looks around the area for a moment before responding.

"I've been ordered to orchestrate a withdrawal. That's a little hard to do with you and your men where you are. So i'll make you a deal. You and your men will get to walk across our lines and return home. Deal?" The man holds out a hand for me to shake but I just stare at it.

"By withdraw you mean you're moving your lines back. Probably because my friends are trying to link up with us." I give him a predatory grin. "I think we'll stay. We wouldn't want to disappoint our reinforcements now would we?" He glares at me a moment before shrugging.

"Very well then. Can I get the name of the commander who led their soldiers to such pointless death?" I nod.

"Of course. Just ask who sent them." I leave after pointing out the rows of now rotting corpses.

3/18/1441

The sounds of artillery hitting their targets is getting closer. It's good to know its ours. Putting the spyglass away I turn to the remains of my company. We'd spent the last couple days making a smaller trench circle inside the old one. It took a lot of work but now we had a place to fight in where we don't have to worry about tripping over the dead.

And now that we could practically see our relief coming to our aid we didn't mind the extra work. Looking towards where the Alliance is attempting to make a breakthrough I then look at where the feds were preparing to launch another assault. This time they wouldn't stop. I could see the glimmer of a knights armor and knew they had decided to finish us off.

"Don't waste your ammo on the knight. Take out the general infantry and wait for the knight to get in close. Aim for the gaps in their armor and they should die like any other man."

Nods from all. Alpha squad almost made up the majority of the company now. Ten out of the twenty-four were my squad. Should feel proud but then I look at squads bravo and delta. I could see the look their sargents gave me. It was one of pity.

Hearing the whistle signaling the confederate assault we all got to our stations. Standing so only our heads and rifles stood above the trench we knew we couldn't allow them anywhere near the center of our new lines. That's were the wounded lay. Some of them gave encouragement from where they lay but most of them were far too weak to speak.

Aim, fire, pull back bolt, repeat. We do this again and again and a hundred feds die. Then a hundred more charge over their fallen comrades. Sone we run out of ammo again and the only thing left to do is wait for them to get closer. Gripping my new pair of pistols i'd gotten from some confederate soldiers I grin. Oh the irony, killed by the very guns meant to keep you safe.

When they get into range I see the knight leading the charge. His silver armor nearly blinded me when the light caught his armor. Shooting the soldiers to his side I make sure when he gets to us he's alone. Ethir he doesn't know or he doesn't care, since he's only response is to run faster and outpace his support. My grin turns into a smile as the realization hits me.

Quickly discarding my spent pistols I draw my sword and back up. The knight sees the opening in our line and makes a beeline for it. When he gets here he jumps right in and makes to run me through with his sword. Instead the CAs on his flanks stab at his exposed armpits. His swing is stopped mid-air and I can see him struggling to lower his sword in my head. Finally he slumps down and we prepare to meet the charge of the real threat.

Feds pour into our outer trench and soon I hear them swearing as smoke begins filling their position. We'd left our smoke grenades behind as gifts. We figured we'd give them a leg up in this fight with their very own smoke screen. Coughing and confused soldiers make their way to our new lines. We'd made four lines for them to get to us and now they funneled through like lambs to slaughter.

Some of their smarter friends had climbed out of the trench to get a height advantage over us. If all of us had been out of ammo that would have worked out quite well for them. As it is the ones i'd told to save their ammo no used them to gun down the soldiers leaving the safety of the trench. With any luck no one will try that again.

Time becomes a blur of swords and rifle butts. The feds can only come at us four at a time of they don't leave the trench and we make short work of them. Grabbing a fallen soldier's rifle I thank them for delivering it to us. Then I raise it and fire at another squad trying to get above us. Guess there was no point hoping they'd just stay in the kill box we'd made for them. I scavenge the fallen attackers for ammo and am followed by any other CA not currently fighting.

Refilling on ammo we're ready when more and more feds try going over the top. There were too many. Eventually a couple manage to return fire and more CAs fall dead or dying. Those who got a shot off don't live long enough to celebrate, yet more come to replace them. One jumps down into the trench but before he can do anything I shoot him through the side of his head and he goes down. Before I can get a new target one finds me.

A bullet rips through my left shoulder and I fall on my back from the force of the impact. Bracing my rifle on the ground I fire at the first head that pops into view. With one arm my aim is atrocious. The bullet comes nowhere near the head and the man it belongs to heads straight for me. Getting up I ditch the rifle and draw my sword in time to cut the man down. Idot should of just shot me.

Feds were pouring over us now. Even the four kill lanes were being overrun by the weight of numbers and now they were pouring in over the top as well. A slash here and a thrust there sends more and more feds to their death. Yet while they get more numerous I can feel my body begin to give out. I was tired, and I will die here among my brothers and sisters. Not a bad way to go really.

Before I clock out though i'll make sure to take a few more with me. Another slash and a confederate soldier falls. Another body to add to the pile. Pain runs through me as a bayonet slices the back of my leg. Instinctively I twist my body and thrust my sword out. The woman who was inches away from skewering me goes to her knees with my sword in her gut.

Getting up with no small amount of effort i'm barely able to parry a sword. Slashing out I take it's owners arm and look over to see alpha five get made into a pincushion by four confederate soldiers. Anger fills me and soon all thoughts of pain or exhaustion vanish. Yelling out like a madman I bullrush them. Two are dead before they know what's happening and the rest disintegrate under my rage fueled assault.

I look at the remains of five. All the times we'd hung out at a bar or trained together goes through my mind in an instant and I feel tears start to well up. Gripping my sword I bellow out a blood curdling warcry and charge through one of the kill lanes that was about to be overrun completely. I plow through them with such furry that by the time I reach the other side i'm drenched in blood.

Now that i'm surrounded by enemies I simply swing my sword in all directions like a madman. There is no meaning to my stance, no efficiency in my strikes, just raw fury. Soldier after soldier is cut down because they had the misfortune of being near me. I knew i'd been cut and stabbed several times but I no longer cared. All I wanted to do was avenge my friend, and to do that i'd need to kill a lot of feds.

Thankfully they'd all packed into our old trench and had been waiting their turn to attack us. For most they'd never get that turn as my sword is used more like a hammer to smash through their skulls or take chunks out of their sides. Some of them scream at the sight of me, and soon i'm grabbing a young man who's trying to run away. I drag him back into the trench and thrust my sword through his chest.

Getting up I look for my next target but there were none. Not a living thing remained in the outer trench. I calm down as the rage slowly leaves my body. As it does it's replaced by unbearable pain. I fall to ground and feel the weight of the world fall off my shoulders. Let someone else take command of this battle, it was time for me to rest.

Chapter 20
The Price Of Victory
Jade

3/29/1441

The fifth company of the twenty-first regiment. They'd been cut off and written for dead until observers had seen their defencive positions. After that Water's army lead charge after charge in an attempt to rescue them. Headless of loses and with little support from Alliance personnel they managed to breakthrough and link up with their allies. What they found shocked them to the very core of their beings.

Eighty-one members of the Combined Arms had been cut off behind enemy lines for almost a month. The fact they lasted that long with their defences only being dirt was a testament to their skills. At least that's what the newspapers have been saying. In reality this was the single greatest loss in CA history. By the time relief arrived only twenty-one were still alive and of those fourteen were heavily wounded. Yet that's not what had shocked the soldiers that came to their rescue.

What had scared them was number of enemy dead all around the area the company had made their stand. Well over a thousand were found dead out in the open, those who hadn't made it to the improvised trench circle the company had made. They were the lucky ones. The first thing Water's soldiers saw when they entered the trench was in their own words. "A butchers shop."
Soldiers had been ripped to shreds by swords or stabbed several times by knives. Some men had gigantic holes in their

chests that made it look like they'd been hit by a cannon. Others looked like they'd been through a meat grinder. Among all the carnage they found the first living being in there.

At first they had thought the CA covered head to toe in gore was dead but then they saw his chest rising slowly. The man was alive and most of the gore was not his. He had suffered a hundred different wounds all over his body and even now he's probably on an ice cold table in a bone white room. No one can guess if sgt Green will live but no matter what he'll not be known by that name anymore.

Prisoners taken after that had surrendered the moment they saw CAs. They all begged not to have to face the berserker. If the newspaper was to be believed then Conner had lost it in that trench and now the entire Confederation feared his might! Since I was given access to actual reports I can say that their not far off. Conner had lost it. According to other survivors he had seen one of his squad get killed and just went mad. He'd cut through the enemy and didn't seem fazed by anything. All he did was hunt every remaining confederate soldier in the trenches. The others had wanted to help but worried that he'd not recognize friend from foe in his blood rage.

And from what i've looked into that's the only explanation I could find that explained things. History books talk about warriors of old that would be driven to such rage that even mortal wounds didn't slow them down. They'd charge headlong into their enemies and take scores of them down. It's said that these warriors were called berserkers. In that regards the feds had named him appropriately.

The news of course has loved this. Water is the first island in the war to throw off the invasion force the feds had sent. Now it was also a birthplace of a hero. With the reports they had they hardly needed to change anything and still people thought they were making it up at first. Then the pictures started appearing in the news. Pictures Water had released to prove the bravery of their Piratenjagers.

No one doubted the news anymore and now the Combined Arms found that their mere presence sent fear to enemy ranks. Now every company may have the wild berserker that could kill whole battalions single handed. In fact the whole Alliance has gotten a bit of hero worship when it comes to CAs as well. Somehow I don't think my father will mind this.

One thing I do mind is the audacity of the Alliance! If they had supported Water then who knows how many lives would of been saved. We may still have a company and that man they call a berserker wouldn't be fighting for his life right now. And now they dare to call him an Alliance hero? The council had dismissed his deeds as falsified reports until Water's military released photos to the press.

Those old farts know nothing of war and had the nerve to say the soldiers who were dieing to keep them in their cozy seats were liars. Their lucky I wasn't in their or i'd show them what a berserker was. Hell our representative had to excuse himself because he feared he'd start bloodbath. I'm sure even my oh so diplomatic father wasn't pleased to hear his soldiers dishonored in such a way.

The thought of my father brings Conner's to my mind. I wonder what he thinks of his son now. His kid was on the other side of the Alliance beaten bloody. Does he even care?

He didn't when his son was captured so why should he when he's nice and safe in a hospital. I may have issues with how my father operates but at the very least I know he loves me. I wonder if Conner can say the same.

Enough thinking about the war. I have a test to study for and a mountain of homework that needs doing. How could I look Conner or the others in the eyes if I let my grades slip. A couple tears drip down as I pick up a frame with a photo of us all together on it. It was taken shortly after we'd all arrived. Samantha had insisted we all take one together to commemorate our first day of classes. For far too many of them it's now the last photo they'll ever be in.

Chapter 21
Reform
Conner

6/14/1441

Being wheeled into the room I attempt a bow in my chair but his majesty waves his hand.

"No need for formalities. I didn't call you here to waste your time after all." I raise my head and take a moment to admire his office. It was simple yet elegant and had a way of making me feel at home.

"You could never waste my time your grace." He gives me a sad smile as he dismisses the aid that had been wheeling me around the palace.

"First off thank you for what you and your company has done. Every one of you is a hero in my book" I stay silent, my body grew cold just thinking about it. "I've been looking for a way to properly award you all for your service and after much deliberation i've come to a decision." I shake my head. "There is no reward required. Knowing our sacrifice had meaning is the greatest gift we can get." He nods.

"That may be but I still find an award is needed to properly express my gratitude." I lean back and wait for him to continue. "The reserve company is going to be used to refill yours to full strength. Of course this will be the last time your regiment is liable to get reinforcements." I look down at the floor. So many dead, all around me… "Of course Captain Steel will no longer be able to command."

Captain Steel. He lost both his legs when a grenade shredded them to bits. By the time healing magic could be applied the limbs had died and had to be removed. He'd be a field commander again and that means i'll have to fill his shoes as the next in line. Closing my eyes I can see his broken body being carried to safety. I followed after him and we went into that tent of horror.

"I wished to give your first orders as Captain in person." I shove my inner thoughts to the side. My king had need of me, I can mourn later. "The UIA is getting pounded hard but we need to secure the Northern border before we can help them." He hands me a file from his desk and I take a moment to look it over.

The operation name was Storm. It came in two stages. First Alliance ships would conduct thunder attacks on confederate supply lines to hinder their operational abilities in the region. Phase two is where the lighting comes into play. A large scale relief of the islands currently under assault.

Reading deeper into the file I could see the plan of attack form in my mind. The plan is to go to Pearl first since it's closest to the Imperiums border. Commandos will land first and clear landing zones or take out defensive positions. That's where the twenty-first comes in. After that the priority will be to link up with allied forces and repel the invaders.

Once Pearl has been secured the task force will gather as much supplies and personnel as they can get and continue down the border. The end goal is to not only to kick the feds out of our waters and get into position for the winter. We'd been blessed/cursed with a late winter this year but that was not going to last.

Depending on how bad the winter is the war could die down for a couple months. If that happens then the task force would have plenty of time to rest and refit while also getting more resources to aid the UIA. If things went according to plan then we can fully commit to an offencive and end the war. Of course that was if it went according to plan. We'd have less then a month to secure each island and while we'd be able to replenish infantry, any ships lost would take time to replace.

Closing the folder I hand it back to his majesty. Shaking my head I state the facts.
"Unless the feds allow it, this plan will never succeed." His face turns grim as he nods at my words.
"It's a fools plan for sure, but it's the only one the council was able to agree on. They expect you guys to kick the feds back across the border and force them to sign a peace before the winter feasts begin."

Winter feasts...The mere mention of it brings memories of large turkey dinners and sharing gifts with loved ones. It's a time where we all get together and pay our respects to our ancestors. The idea that this war could be over by then actually brings a smile to my face but before it can get to big it turns into a frown. Only a fool would think this plan could work, and only an idiot would think that if it did the feds would roll over.

"What do you wish of us my lord?" In the end no other question matters. The thoughts about turkey dinners disappear as I stare at my king to tell me why me and my company are die.
"I expect Pearl to be secured quickly enough. After that I can only ask that you attempt to conserve your forces for next year. I have a feeling that we'll need every CA we can get before the wars over." Nodding to his orders I look up at

him and salute. Turning to leave I catch my father's eyes staring after me. Opening the door I flash him the best smile I can muster and head out.

6/18/1441

Leaning heavily on my cane I stare at the rows of swords sticking from the ground. Each sword was made of stone and had both a hat on their hilt and a plake where it's blade met the ground. They were the eighty men and woman that died so far from home. With them lay four members of my own squad. Walking down the rows I see medals and flowers spread around the graves, the last gifts to the dead.

Arriving to section A I kneel down to the four grave markers. Peter Grey, Mike West, Steve Jones, Tony Marks. All four of these men had died with valor and I should be able to rest easy knowing that they can join their ancestors with their heads held high. Yet all I feel is pain. Pain from the guilt of knowing that their deaths are on my shoulders. If i'd noticed the feds trap or fought a little harder then we'd all be drinking together right now. Mike and Peter would be flirting with the staff, Steve would be apologizing for them, and Tony would stand ready should any of the squad start a fight and need treatment.

These were now some of the last memories I have of these great men. They are far too few and I can only wonder at the lost stories and adventures. We made a great team… no we made a great family. All of us together were on top of the world when we'd gotten our new uniforms.

Taking out my sgt stripes I lay them in front of Tony's grave. "I made captain. Steel lost his legs so now i'm in charge. Of

course that means Marcus is in charge of Alpha now. If you were here you'd probably die laughing." Looking towards the heavens I hold back the tears welling up.
"You were a damn good medic Tony. I'm sure we'll have a hard time without you but I swear we won't be joining you too soon. Not until we finish what we started with you. When we do join up again we'll have a drink and catch up. I'm sure i'll have more stories to tell."

Rising to my feet I give the grave a warm smile. Walking away I list the name of every soldier… No of every brother and sister that I pass. When I reach the final grave marker I feel the pitter patter of rain and look back to get a good look at the final resting place of so many of my family.

"Till we meet again."

6/23/1441

Looking over my company I see few familiar faces. The survivors of Water are formed into the first squad with the rest being spread out to be in charge of the new squads. These new member were not green per say, all of them had completed CA training and had continued that training while awaiting their formation into a company. Unfortunately that would never come and now their a part of the fifth.

They have the best training I can hope for but it'd be foolish of me not to remember that none of them have seen action. Guess it doesn't really matter in the end. They'll soon be getting all the experience they could want. It's my job to ensure they get to live long enough to use that experience.

"Squad leaders! Front and center." Immediately ten people

come up to the front of the company. Looking over I see the tired looking Marcus giving a grin. He'd stepped up to being squad lead but that doesn't mean he'd enjoyed it. "The Alliance has come up with a hairbrained scheme that is in the realm of impossible. Thankfully for them they had the intelligence to call us in." Ash nods her head a couple times and her squad, mostly new, smile at the encouragement. "Our job is a simple one by our standards. All we have to do is clear a place for the Alliance to land." Looking again at my company I finish my little speech on a more sober tone. "The feds think they can come and take our lands, it's up to us to remind them that war isn't the same as counting money."

Some of the new members cheer, but the old guard knew what they were up against. The feds are not incompetent and will no doubt be expecting an attack. Even discounting their naval presence they'll have a force ready to intercept any landing attempts. Considering how easy it was for us on defence I can't imagine any of the veterans to be thrilled about being on the offense. We'll need every ounce of skill and more then a little luck.

Chapter 22
Pearl
Conner

8/11/1441

0200

Looking over the squad leaders I tap the map on the wall. The island named Pearl had a lot of natural beauty. Lush tropical forests and beaches, hills and well marked hiking trails, cities lit up by lights at night. Even on a piece of paper the island seems grand and full of splendor. What I was tapping was a small private beach.

The property is owned by the governor's family and has been in their position for generations. From the beach you could take a paved trail through the forest until you come upon their manor. Connecting the manor to the capital of Legburg was a single railway with a luxury train. Command hadn't expected that it all be intact but when the airships scouted the island out they were able to confirm that the manor and the train were intact.

Another thing the airships reported was that most of the island was under enemy control. The only remaining cities flying Alliance colors was the capital and its sister city of Steamburg. The capital was well known as the city of lights but it being under allied control is surprising. The city serves as the main rail hub and was also a major tourist location. Most figured the local government would rather surrender then risk damaging such an important city.

If it's still in our control then it's probably thanks to Steamburg. They were a little out of the way but that meant it was perfect for their local military. Wouldn't want soldiers to scare the tourists away. Under normal circumstances i'd say they were fools but because of its remote location they had the fortune to be left alone by the feds. Even a mob can turn a city into a fortress if given enough time and this was a city full of soldiers. The report had mentioned a large body of troops outside the city so it's not hard to get a picture.

The feds probably want to take out the army before taking the capital. No one wants to march on a city with an enemy army at their back. Even if Legburg surrendered it'd be easy for the army in Steamburg to sally forth and do some damage. Not to mention that even if the local governor surrendered that didn't mean that the army would. A counter attack is possible and if so then they'd become a major thorn in the fed's defence plan. All this gave good signs for an invasion.

"As you can see command wants to give us a break. Our job is to make sure the beach is clear and make sure the feds haven't left any surprises for us." I trace my finger over the forest past the beach. "After making sure the beach is clear command wants us to act as vanguard through the forest. Our objective is the governor's family's manor. More specifically the train connecting it to the capital." Dragging my finger across the railroad I trace it all the way to the capital. "From there we lead the charge to the capital. Make sure they haven't run out of tea and head to Steamburg's aid." I finish by tapping the only other city with a blue pin in it. "Any questions?" Sam raises a hand. Nodding towards her I wonder how she's fitting in as delta one.
"What defences have the airships spotted on the beach?" I give her a tired shrug.
"Report says they found no indication of defences. Command thinks we got the feds napping, I think our eyes in the sky need glasses. I can't imgen the feds leaving such an obvious gap in their defences." All over the islands costs were bunkers or trench lines. They didn't come here to leave at the first sign of a fight, so I can't see why they'd leave a

gap.

"My best guess is that they hid their defences in the forests. If that's the case then we'll be in for a hard fight with no cover." Ash nods.

"Shouldn't be too difficult. All we have to do is lunch smokes when we get close. With the new mark III rifles we got we should be able to get a screen up long before we come into range."

We all smile at the mention of the mark III. CA command had added the rifle to our standard kit and the rifle was the best on the market. Same range and ammo as the mark I with a detachable scope and grenade launcher. It was made to be as reliable as the mark I with the range and power of the mark II sniper variant. With only a few tests of the thing we can't say for certain that that's true but we loved firing them and won't be giving them back.

"Working on the idea of a smokescreen I remind all of you to keep your squads in check. I don't want friendly fire on the beach, so just take the time to get to the forest." Markus taps a flare gun on his hip.

"And if the beach is too crowded we let them know." I nod.

"Unless we send up the warning then the first wave of Alliance marines will hit the beach at 0600. We'll have roughly half an hour on the beach before that happens so don't waste time if you can avoid it." Everyone nods. After waiting a couple seconds I confirm that no one else has any questions. "Ok dismissed. We'll meet up at 0500 to head ashore."

0400

Finishing my letter I put it in the sack to await until it can be sent. It'll probably be after the battle before any mail will be sent out. Alliance command was insane to think this would be an easy fight. Some of the officers had even told me I was lucky to be one of the first to get to take a trip to the beach.

The letter to CA command is nothing more than a report of my unit's status. It also contains my unit's opinion of the new rifle. It is not an understatement that all of us look forward to seeing it in action. Indeed most of the report is filled with praise for the design.

The letters to my family are filled with hpe and joy. Joy to see the war moving on and hope to see them again. I send them all that i've experienced while i've been away, the good and the bad. Among the letter is a picture of me and the remains of my class. Not a single one of us is saluting. Some of us have our arms wrapped around each other while others are making faces or in odd poses. I myself am standing back to back with Markus with Sam kneeling in front of us. We all look genuinely happy, something none of us thought would be possible after Water.

Getting up I put on my pack and sling my rifle over my shoulder. Taking my sword out for inspection I admire the new blade. Gearboxes work is always a marvel and even though it wasn't the original it looked no different. It's weight was identical to my old one and if anything it unfolded faster than before. Sliding the blade back I place the sword at my hip and head out of my room.

0530

Approaching the beach ten canisters are shot from the boats. A few seconds later the whole beach is obscured by a dense white fog. Using the fog as cover we land. The boat i'm in is filled with alpha squad, and together we get out and start running towards where the forest should be.

A machine gun breaks the silence of the night and its met by several more of the machines as they all fire into the smoke. Normally we'd dive for cover but that would only help us until the smoke cleared. If anyone was still on the beach when the smoke cleared they were as good as dead.

Seeing a break in the smoke I begin seeing trees and behind them soldiers pointing rifles my way. Sliding to a knee I pull the trigger and a 'pop' goes out. From the tip of my rifle the metal canister sends out a it's deadly payload and a heartbeat later a grenade lands behind the enemy. The explosion is short and sweet but leaves nothing standing. Either the enemy is dead or taking cover.

I see alpha break through the smoke and head into the forest. Now small arms fire joins the machine guns and all over the beach I know similar scenes are breaking out. Moving up I leave the smoky beach in favor of the enemy rich forest. I nearly trip over a fed who was taking cover and both of us let out a cry of surprise. I react first and slam the butt of my rifle into their head and he goes down. While I put another grenade in the canister I look around and attempt to get a lay of the battle.

As far as the eye can see is trees and the occasional shape moving through the darkness. The sounds of combat confuse me even more as the only thing I could hear was explosions and machine gun fire. How did Steel manage the unit during battle?

My thoughts are interrupted by a bullet hitting the trunk I was using as cover. Seeing the shape of the man I fire my grenade at them. The shape falls back as their hit by the force of the grenade. Before the poor bastard can confirm that their alive the grenade goes off. Another explosion rips through the din of battle and for a moment the area is lit up.

Seeing a full platoon in the vicinity of the grenade I decide not to go in that particular direction. Instead I head towards where I can see a machine gun lighting up the beach. Taking off the canister I latch it to my belt and open fire on the machine gun post. The light of the machine gun quickly fades as the gunner dives for cover. There was little chance I actually hit them but sometimes suppressing fire is just as good.

I don't wait for their counter fire. Instead I charge forward and find myself falling down in the darkness. Landing hard on my hands and knees I instinctively roll to the side. A bayonet buries itself where I lay not a moment before. Firing blindly at the assailant I know i've fallen in one of their trenches. Attempting to get up i'm hit hard by the butt of a rifle. Falling to the ground yet again I prepare to feel the pain of a bayonet but it never comes. Getting up I see the man that was about to kill me dead. Looking around I see a couple members of bravo laying down covering fire for me.

Taking this opportunity I get up and proceed through the trench. Running along the trench I find several dead soldiers and make a mental note to award bravo for their marksmanship. Coming up to a underground room I toss a grenade inside. Unlike the high explosive ones i've been using for the rifle this is one of my shrapnel grenades. Five seconds after i'd tossed it the grenade goes off and I walk into the room.

Inside I find a lit room that nearly blinds me. After my eyes adjust I see it was a mostly empty observation post. The few occpents hat had maintained their position now lay dead on the floor. Not seeing another exit I leave the way I came in and proceed down the line. I see a couple figures grappling on the ground and get closer to see bravo one is currently beating the crap out of a unfourtantant fed. Seeing a couple of the man's friends coming to his aid I fire at them. They quickly fall from my assault and not long after bravo one finishes her gruesome job. She nods to me and together we march through the trench while her squad provides covering fire from above us.

Reloading I see bravo has slung her rifle over her back in favor of her sword and pistol. She uses the former to dispatch a fed who appeared out of the darkness. Before I can thank her another couple feds come into sight and I shoot them down. Glancing above me I see that the rest of bravo is firing at unseen enemies. Probably reserves coming up to reinforce the first line.

Arriving at a bunker I nod to bravo one and she tosses a grenade inside. Immediately after it goes off she's inside and I hear her pistol making short work of whoever remained standing. I myself am forced to enter the bunker when more and more feds fire on my position. Ducking inside I see bravo one moving a machine gun towards the door. Ditching my rifle I help her and we set it up just in time to meet the charge of confederate soldiers.

The roar of the machine gun deafens me and the sight of a squad of soldiers being cut down leaves a nasty taste in my mouth. Not long after a grenade comes into the bunker and I slap it outside. Following the explosion on it's heels I come out of the bunker and draw my blade. As it unfolds I imbed it inside a woman who was just recovering from the grenade. Taking the blade out I use the momentum to swing into another soldier's neck. The man's head sails into the darkness and his comrades race to avenge him. Even four on one i'm confident in my skills with a blade and dispatch three of them in short order. The last parries my attack and nearly guts me with their counter. Dodging to the side I seperate their arm from their body and they go down screaming in pain.

Bravo one comes out of the bunker and fires my rifle at another soldier about to shoot me. Nodding towards her she passes me my rifle and I put my sword away. The rest of bravo is getting inside the trench, unable to stay above with the threat of reinforcements. Bravo one quickly dispatches two of them to get the machine gun and move it out here. They head inside the bunker and when they come out the first rays of sunlight begin to appear.

Checking my watch I see that the marines should be arriving in the nest few minutes. They'll be getting to us when the sun is up and the risk of friendly fire is low. Before then though we must secure our position. I leave bravo to hold this section of the trench and head farther along the line. I meet a squad on their way to attack bravo from the side and I drive them off with my rifle.

Following the squad as they retreat delta reveals themselves. They burst out of a bunker and before the feds can react their cut down. Soon after the squad takes out a machine gun and begins setting it up to repel counter attacks. With the light coming in they'll soon realize how small a force is currently here and attack. Nodding to delta as I pass I can't stop a smile from forming on my lips. Delta was mostly new blood so seeing them all in one piece and handling themselves has to be a good sign.

Past delta the trench is mostly empty. Except for the occasional squad of mine I can't seem to find any living enemies. Looking over the trench I try and make out any large formations moving towards us. Not seeing any I look the opposite direction to see marines piling onto the beach. They were coming in a platoon at a time and in only a couple minutes the trench was filled with them.

Once they've secured the trench I can see engineers setting up a temporary port so that larger ships can bring in artillery and supplies. They'll also bring in the bulk of the army but if we don't press forward then they'll be sitting ducks on the beach. Seeing one of my men nearby I grab him and tell him to gather the rest of the company as fast as he can. He nods and heads back to his squad. He takes three others and they split up to round up the company.

Looking deeper into the forest I wonder how much time they'll give us before they counter. They know we'll be landing more and more units until we can simply overwhelm them with numbers. Since they haven't launched a counterattack that means either their ok with us gathering here or that they didn't think they'd be able to take and hold our position. As much as i'd like the later option to be true I have to assume that their waiting for us to land as many assets as possible before bombarding our position. At least that's what i'd do in their shoes.

Seeing a marine setting up a radio I head over to him. He looks over to me and without a word hands me the mike. I tell him to get me in contact with command and he turns some knobs and flips a switch. Hearing a gruff old voice ask for my identification I give my name and rank. After a moment another voice comes over the line.

"Captain Green. It's good to hear from you. We got concerned when we started to hear your fight. Hope it wasn't too much trouble over there." I look around me at all the dead confederate soldiers and the marines changing the trench to face the proper direction.
"Nothing we couldn't handle sir. I'm regrouping my company as we speak and believe we need to push the feds out of artillery range of the beach as fast as possible sir." I take off my pack and dig through it to get out a map of the island. Spreading it out on the ground I barely hear the radio.
"Agreed captain, but we are planning to wait until we can get an idea of the enemy defences before launching an attack. Are you able to offer assistance?" By now four squads had formed around me and I glance at them. No casualties so far.
"Affirmative sir. With your leave we can use our flares to light up enemy position for naval bombardment sir." A moment's pause. No doubt looking over a similar map as me.
"Understood captain. We'll wait ten after the flare is spotted before commencing bombardment. Be advised that the fleet will only offer minimal support." Glancing behind me I see the rest of the company has gathered. The few missing are ethir dead or wounded.
"Roger that sir. Will commence recon immediately. Captain Green over and out."

Giving the mike back to the marine I turn to my company.

We were cramped into the trench but I could tell that most of them had made it through. Giving them the best once over I could I saw many of them had minor wounds here and there. They my side of the conversation and know what I need without asking.

Any squad with more than four men down disperse to aid the marines. The reaming squad leaders eye each other before delta and bravo step forward. Each squad had no dead and only minor wounds. Bravo had experience but very little when it came to recon operations. Delta had mostly fresh faces with a couple vets. They were clearly eager to prove themselves which made me wonder if they should be the ones to go.

Thinking it over for a second I nod toward delta. They have only slightly less experience than us when it came to this kind of mission so there's no reason to keep them here. Bravo however had a wealth of experience when it came to defence. Like the other survivors of Water they spent most of the time being on the defensive so keeping them back would be better.

As they smile and head off to complete their task I have no doubts that they'll complete it. They have proven themselves able in combat and so long as they remember their training this will be an easy mission. The hardest part will be when it comes time to withdraw. Even the best training in the world can't make you bulletproof and retreating under enemy fire will be a true test for them. I can only hope they all live to tell tales of this day to their children.

0720

Seeing ten flares light up the enemy positions I take out my watch. They have ten minutes to vacate the area before the navy does it's best to level it. After that the marines will advance to take the forest. While they work to secure the forest me and my company is to make a beeline for the governor's manor. All future plans depend on the condition of the rail line there.

If it's intact then we can send reinforcements straight to the capital. If not then the glorious campaign that'll kick the feds out of our waters and force a end to the war will end before the first snow. Not that I or anyone with any sense expected it to work at all. The best we can hope for is taking Pearl and maybe one other island. The rest will have to hold on through winter.

Thinking of winter reminds me of the almost unbearable heat. The sun had barely risen and already people were wiping away sweat and drinking deeply from their canteens. I had been told that it was hotter up hear but nothing could of prepared me for this heat. Almost makes me wish winter would hurry up.

Seeing ten minutes on my watch had passed I hear the far off booms of the naval guns. Not long after the forest is lit up as the shells land and explode. For several minutes we all watch as the tropical forest reduced to ash and craters. The areas around where the flares had been set off no longer was a forest. In their place we could now clearly see craters and broken timber. Even furthur around we could see the now exposed trenches and the gun nests where soldiers prepared for the infantry assault that would follow.

The marines oblige them as a series of whistle tell them to go over the top. The surviving machine guns open up along

with the riflemen that had remained mostly unharmed from the bombardment. Marines fell in droves but they continued their push. Once they got into range grenades went flying and silenced the machine guns while other units took shelter in the craters the navy had provided them.
From the gap the naval bombardment had made the marines poured in. Once the machine guns went silent the infantry was forced to retreat or be annihilated by the assaulting force. While the enemy retreated the marines occupied their former positions and prepared new defences. While they did that the fresh army divisions that had been crowding the beach went into action. They went past my company as we reunited with delta and charged over the marines who hollered encouragement. While the marines had expanded a gap the army's job was to make a breach for my unit to go through.

Even through delta looked worse for ware I couldn't afford to leave a tenth of my forces behind and we all march forward. The army was hurling themselves against the enemy and while they were taking heavy losses they were making progress. By the time my company arrives the army had forced a breach and were working to force the enemy to withdraw again. As much as i'd like to help them I have my own mission and press past them. Once we get over the third line we meet obstacles almost immediately. We passed the army who were fighting tooth and nail with the enemy and practically ran into the enemies reinforcements.

From the number I could see I guess them to be battalion strength. Thankfully their as surprised by us as we are by them and my company gets off the first strike. We split into squads immediately with me joining charlie. Each squad takes to the trees as cover and don't bother trying to out shoot the enemy. Grenades go flying and the whole area goes up into fire as they blow up all over the place. Trees are blown apart causing more shrapnel to spread and some to catch fire. Soon black smoke starts to fill our eyes with tears but still we fight on. The enemy pours fire into our cover and I see one man huddling behind a tree as it's ripped to shreds by rifle fire. Yet as quickly as it began the engagement ends.

The enemy withdraws and we press forward. Not far in we are again stopped by what can only be a rearguard unit. Past them I see horses carting away artillery pieces and wagons laden with wounded. I order whoever still has grenades for our rifles to fire them at the artillery and soon after the big guns are peppered by explosions. Many of the poor animals lugging the weapons off are killed, the unfortunate survivors are left to cry in pain as shrapnel rips through their flesh.

The guns and horses are quickly abandoned in favor of carting off the wounded. I order a ceasefire and soon the feds get the message. They don't mess with us and they can cart their wounded off. Better that way for both of us as I have neither the time nor the ability to take prisoners. I do however insure that not a single wounded horse remains living longer than necessary. It takes time but not doing so would be far too cruel to me. The poor animals are put out of their misery and I pray to my ancestors for forgiveness. Such noble beasts should not be slaughtered in such a way.

After the horses are dealt with we move on. Through the forest we can see the main road that leads to the manor but dare not travel on it. Even being within seeing distance of a road puts us all on edge. This is where enemy artillery will fire to halt the armies advance. Unfortunately for us all we don't have a choice. We can't risk missing the manor because we were too deep in the woods. Even this far away was a risk but any closer would leave us far too exposed.

Soon one of the squads spots the manor and not long after we all fan out around it. From our position we can see the back and side but most of the front was obscured. What we could see was several soldiers running around carrying boxes of documents while others were clearly preparing explosives. A finely dressed man was howling at the soldiers to hurry up and charly one taps my shoulder.

"Sir if i'm not mistaken that's general Martins. He's a confederate big shot who called for a the army to get more funding." I look the old man over.

Plum and full of anger the man hardly screamed enemy let alone general. If it wasn't anyone else i'd ask them if they were blind. Considering the source of this information was the person who until recently had been my number three I decide that the fat man most be who she says. Even through his attire was nothing but a robe I determined to either kill or capture the man.

Besides the 'general' my main priority is the train. From where I am I can see it being loaded with expensive looking paintings and furniture as well as documents. The man clearly had his values in check as he made sure to leave enough room in the last train car for himself and several servants. I can only pity the poor bastard in charge of the soldiers that probably think their position is about to be overrun. Wait that's it!

Quickly relaying orders to my squad leaders I tell them my plan. Not long after they all give their affirmative. As the last of the servants get aboard the train and the general prepares to embark himself I howl out for the order to charge. Three squads are at the train before the soldiers can react and the rest of us appear and raise our rifles at the tired soldiers. Up until now they had been running around carrying furniture and documents to a train. The general calls for the soldiers to fire but they look to another man.

A major who looked far too professional to be working under the fat general looks around at all of us. In his mind he's seeing what I see. Very little odds of success and high odds of failure. If they fought they were at a clear disadvantage and could only hope to take some of us with them. They had been caught off guard and at a time when many of them were not in any shape for a fight. The general may not see it but the major clearly does. With a sigh he lowers his head and raises his hands. Shortly after the rest of the soldiers do as well.

The general screams abuse but is silenced by a couple members of foxtrot who restrain and gag him. The servants and the soldiers all seem in a better mood after this even as their striped of their weapons and lined up against the train. While the radio is set up the rest of the company sets up a perimeter around the manor. We were likely to meet the enemy before relief arrives.

Once the radio is up and running I give a quick report of the situation. The other side of the line pauses to breathe a sigh of relief before congratulating me. The feds were falling back faster than we could take their positions and friendly forces were already on their way to link up with us. Apparently the operation had gone well even though enemy resistance was greater than expected.

Thinking back to how command had thought the feds had

left a gap for us to exploit I can't help but look at the fat general who was trying to bite through his gag. This victory was far from a clean one and I doubt it'll get any easier. Just taking the train and manor wasn't the end. Now we would have to fight to hold what we've taken and attempt to link up with whatever allied forces are still fighting. We were in for a tough fight.

8/16/1441
1200

Looking over the six coffins I can't help but wonder if they needed to die. Perhaps if I had insisted that the forest needed a bombardment before we landed or if I had ordered the smoke screen sooner. Any of these actions may have left at least some of these coffins unnecessary. Shaking my head I dismiss such thoughts. If I allow my mind to wander down that dark path i'll be unable to lead my unit and far more will die. I must remain calm and in control.

A hand rests on my shoulder. Turning I see Markus and Sam. Both of them give me half hearted smiles.
"What are you two doing here? You should be with your squads." Markus shrugs and Sam sighs.
"And so we are. You were our sargent long before you were our captain, and our friend before both." I turn back to the coffins.
"Friends eh? I don't even know the names of any of these guys. I used to be able to call out our entire class by name and knew more than a few of their families. Now I don't even bother remembering anyone unless they are a squad leader." Markus lets his hand drop and Sam goes over to the coffins. Placing a hand on one she looks over to me.
"Her name was Margaret. She was twenty years old and had

two younger sisters who she looked out for. Before we left she was late to our first briefing because one of her sisters wouldn't let her leave." Turning to me I see the tears hiding at the edges of her eyes.

"I'm sorry Sam. I forgot this was your first command. How'd she die?" Her eyes take on a vacant look as if she's reliving the event.

"It was when we met that battalion before reaching the manor. She'd taken cover behind a rock and was returning fire when a grenade landed next to her. I barely had time to shout a warning before it went off." Markus goes over to two of the coffins and places his hands on them both.

"These two knuckleheads were nothing but trouble. They were brothers that wouldn't stop trying to one up each other. I was going to transfer one of them to echo but decided against it. Now their poor parents are going to get two flags instead of one." He turns to stare at me. "Was it this bad for you?" I look at both of them. They had appeared happy and full of life before we left for this cursed thing we called war. Now all three of us had the weight of countless deaths on our shoulders.

"At least we can tell their parents they didn't die in vain." Both of them give a solemn nod.

This was only partially true. We'd secured a great victory but that didn't mean the fight was over yet. The feds were on the run while our own forces were beginning to liberate towns and cities that had been occupied. While my company didn't take the train other units did and now a second front has opened at Legburg. We had far too many wounded to be any use in a fight so other divisions were used to link up with the capital. Command had tried to assure me that there would be no fighting in Legburg but I didn't budge. My unit would remain until we finished licking our wounds.

When the first division left they made it halfway before getting stopped at a checkpoint. After several hours of having fighting the feds were driven off but the division had taken heavy losses. While what was left of them had taken up defence of the checkpoint another division was sent up with the train. After securing the checkpoint they again attempted to reach the capital but were again forced to fight a grueling battle. Even now we had yet to reach the capital and even through command has sent another division we all know the same thing will happen again.

At least command isn't pinning all their hopes on the train. With the marines taking charge of the forest the army has been slowly but surely spreading out. For the first couple days the army met only rearguard units that delayed them but yesterday they got into a big battel over a nearby city. It was a place called Ronia that barely met the qualifications to be called a city. It served as the main trading hub for nearby towns and was one of the few places that wasn't advertised as a tourist local.

At first command had wanted the army to secure other more well known cities but field commanders had made it clear Ronia needed to be taken. If they didn't take it then then the army was at risk of making a huge salient that the feds could exploit. If the feds prepared things right then the army would get pincered between port cities where the feds were confirmed to have several divisions and Ronia. As it was command seemed to be taking Ronia seriously. Today three divisions have been ordered to secure Ronia and another two have been ordered to harass the ports. It won't be long until we're called to action again.

The real question was whether we would be sent to try and reach the capital or take Ronia. If I had to choose i'd steer away from Ronia. The feds are going to be dug in and it'll be hell to dig them out. Sheer numbers will be needed to win that battle and that's the type of battle CAs are told to avoid. Of course getting to Legburg won't be easy ethir but if I have to fight somewhere i'd rather fight somewhere where I don't have to worry about civilians.

A runner comes up and hands me a missive. Reading it over I look over to the others and toss it to the ground. They head off to gather their squads while I head to the manor. Wondering where they plan to send us I make my way to the manor. Getting to the big double doors that make the front entrance I see two guards who open the doors once they see me. Saluting to them as I pass I enter the lavish abode of the governor's family.

Expensive furniture and paintings that get bigger and more grand the closer I get to the main hall. Another couple guards are stationed at the entrance to the main hall and they wait to confirm that i'm expected. After a couple minutes they open the door and i'm allowed to enter. The grand hall was probably at once point in time truly great. At the moment any splendor was lost due to the large table with maps strewn over it. The elderly looking men in uniforms didn't add to the decor nor did the rows of desks with radio equipment, pigeons, and telegrams. Where people once gathered to celebrate people now make preparations for war.

One of the older men at the table waves me over and I oblige. I give him a quick salute and he returns it. After he lowers his hand he points to the map on the table. It was a bigger and far more detailed version of the one I carried with me at all times. This one had, among other things, several red and blue flags. He points to Ronia where several flags of both colors were touching each other, then he motions towards the capital. The route there seemed to invite us along but screamed 'trap'.

"We've lost thousands of soldiers just getting halfway to the capital via the train. Even the most optimistic of us says it'll take another couple thousand before we get to Legburg. While that goes on we have the shit show at Ronia. When the vanguard fought there yesterday they met heavy resistance. Not many of them walked away." He looks over to me. His eyes are tired and had dark rings under them. I nod in the direction of the map.
"Where do you want us sir?" He looks over to a different part of the map. Following his eyes I see the town of Steamburg where a single blue flag was surrounded by a sea of red.
"The manor has phone and telegraph lines connecting to most of the major cities. With them we were able to contact the troops at Steamburg and they gave us their situation. They have a full corps getting squished by two army groups. The fact they've lasted this long is nothing less than a miracle."

Looking over to the map where one blue flag stood against the tide of red I shake my head. At best they were outnumbered four to one and yet they still held on. I have to wonder why the feds haven't just used their artillery to bomb them into submission. Even if they had no artillery at all i'd think such a huge numerical advantage would break through. Perhaps we should reevaluate the ability of Pearls military forces.

"They reported that earlier today the forces arrayed against them have diminished. They can't tell how many but we know where their heading." Looking at where Steamburg was it wasn't hard to see. They were just a couple days march from Legburg and even closer is the railroad that we've been trying to use. The two blue flags representing the divisions currently holding at a captured checkpoint suddenly look vulnerable.

"Do you want us to act as a delaying force sir?" Staying at extreme range we should be able to slow them down a bit.

"Getting there isn't the problem. The real problem is that we have to defend the rail line while they just have to cut a single section of it. We want an open battle where we can bloody or destroy their army. To that end we plan on marching on Steamburg." Looking at the map I picture a open battle where soldiers charge at each other until finally meeting in a bloody melee. It wasn't a pretty picture.

"And where does my unit come in sir?"

He taps one of the small towns.

"This little village rests on top of a hill that dominates the area around it for miles. Getting artillery there would be great, hell just getting machine guns would be fine. That's where your unit comes in. You'll go out there with as many machine guns and ammo as you can carry and hold the location until relieved. Once the rest of the divisions get there we'll toute them back to Steamburg and pincer them."

Seeing Steamburg surrounded by red I can see where the plan comes from. Taking out such a large enemy force could very well bring an end to the campaign with plenty of time for us to move on with commands grander goal. If it works it'll be one for the history books at the very least. Of course there's that if. If the plan works than taking Pearl would be an afterthought. Not even the Confederation with all their manpower can lose two army groups and not feel the sting.

Of course if they win then who cares about Steamburg? They could turn around and contain us to the forest. That'll leave the divisions dealing with Ronia trapped and the whole campaign would grind to a halt. In that scenario it wouldn't be a surprise to find a confederate fleet coming to trap us here. Then the Alliance will be the one feeling the pain. Pearl would be lost for sure, but we may find ourselves losing all the border islands if the feds act quickly enough. It was a big risk but it had big rewards.

"We'll keep the hill under our control sir, but everything after that is up to fate." He gives me a galre.
"Fate? You doubt our abilities?" I shake my head.
"No sir. I just don't doubt the enemies."

Chapter 23
Butcher Hill
Conner

8/18/1441
1330

Entering the town I look around and see people coming out to meet us. They stand outside their homes and their shops to see their allies coming to save the day. No more than a hundred people watch us. After a moment an elderly man comes up to me and asks where i'm heading.

"Sorry to tell you but this whole area will be a battlefield soon. You'll want to clear out before the days end." Murmurs erupt from the crowd. From the sounds of it they aren't too keen on leaving.
"I'm sorry young man but we can't leave. This is our home!" I shrug.
"This is war. I'm sure your government will be more than happy to pay reparations after we drive the feds off your island." More mumbling, this time I sense the change in the air. Some of them weren't looking too friendly anymore.
"Well you listen here young man! We didn't ask for this war, so you can go have your battle somewhere else." Some heavy set men walk up to either side of the old man. Others started shuffling children and elderly indoors.
"We didn't ask for the war ethir but here we are. Now I suggest you leave before the shooting starts." The old man squares his shoulders.
"No." I raise an eyebrow at him. He has the stubbornness

that can only come from old age.

"Listen i'm sorry but nothing's gonna change the battles location. Now if we don't use this hill than a lot of good people will die, so please understand when I say we have to ask you to leave." A young man wearing farmers overalls shouts out.

"Nothing good about soldiers! All you ever do is kill. The world would be better off without you." Others begin to cheer him on and he continues. Ethir he doesn't notice my unit getting tense or he doesn't care. "Besides you say you didn't ask for the war but your from Blade right? Everyone knows you lot have been itching for a fight. That's why you've been egging on the imperium in hopes that they'll start a war." I stare at the young man. How many people have died for this shit?

"I'll consider your words as ignorance because of your age. Now go back to your mom." The young man picks up a rock and throws it at me. I swat it out of the air and glare at the old man. "My patience only goes so far. I asked and now i'm telling. Leave." The old man gives me a grin.

"Make us." Poor words.

With a wave of my hand the company breaks into squads and comes towards the few that had remained in the streets. A few resist but in only a matter of minutes all of them are tied up and I look at the now restrained old man. He spits at me and resist the urge to kick his head in. They do realize we are dieing for them right?

"Your being evicted. If I have to say that again i'm just going to start throwing people down the hill." After making sure that they got the message I order them released.

Seeing how easily we were able to subdue them they make the logical decision not to fight back again. They give us dirty looks and more than a few threats but so what? We have a job to do and while I don't like kicking them out of their own homes they have some skewed ideas about how the world works. Antagonise the Imperium into a war? We were already fighting one with them, the rest of the Alliance just didn't want to admit.

Ignoring the snide comments I focus on the battle ahead. Each squad took four machine guns and ammo in abundance. All of that need to be stored and set up. Scouts will be needed to find the enemy. Cooking fires must be lit. So much work. Thinking these thoughts I look around the town.

Several small homes around a center that seems to have served as a market square. Stores and stalls were placed around a simple well. Heading over to the well I look around and see four main entrances to the square with enough eight or so side alleys nestled between buildings. Those side alleys will need to be closed and barricades to block up the main streets. The stalls could be used to block the alleys but we'll have to set up sandbags or something for the main entries.

If we set it up this way we can have two squads stay back here with their machine guns as a fallback line. The rest of us can make the outer homes a makeshift wall. Playing our cards right we'll be able to turn the whole town into a fort. Thirty-two machine guns will turn this town into a death trap if we place them in the right place.

8/19/1441
1500

Looking through a window I can see the enemy soldiers in the distance. From here i'd guess them to be corps strength. Even with my binarclors I can only see blurs in the distance.

Slowly they come into focus and not long after a couple fall over. Zooming out I see my scouting force pop up of nowhere to fire ate extreme range. With the new mark III we have a massive range advantage. The sounds of a struggle rip my attention away from the fight. Looking over to the door to the room i've been using to observe the area I see a young man thrown into the room.

Looking over to the young man I see a couple members of bravo enter. The young man seems familery to me and it takes me a moment before I place his face. Those blue eyes filled with hate, the dirty farmers overalls, and hair the color of straw. He was that little shit from yesterday. Seeing him bound and gagged I couldn't help but wonder what brings him here. Though I can't deny that seeing him ruffed up didn't bring me some joy.

"Now what the hell am I supposed to do with him." I look at Ash as she enters the room. She picks up the young man and slams him against the wall.
"Find this shit rummaging by the well. Figure he came to get some revenge." The young man looks at me and I see the hate in his eyes.
"I doubt this man would poison the well. He loves his home far too much to kill it just so we can't have it. As for why he's here… Why don't we ask?" With some reluctance Ash goes over to undo their gag. He takes a couple deep breaths before snarling at me.
"You basterds! Kicking us out isn't enough for you so now you're tearing down our homes?" Looking at the man I walk over and grab him by the hair. His cries of pain bring me no joy as I shove his head outside the window. Pointing him in the direction of the confederate army I fight the temptation to shove him out.

"You see that massive blob in the distance. That's the feds coming to kill us. Now that you've seen that I hope you'll understand what's about to happen to you." Dragging him away from the window I pass him to Ash. "Toss him out of the town. We aren't running an inn here." Ash smiles as she drags the young man away. He shouts a bit before he's silenced by what i'd guess would be another gag.

Looking out the window again I see my scouts withdrawing. Zooming out I see that the feds have sent out skirmishers. Every time the skirmishers would get ready to fire the scouts leave their range and return fire. Several of the skirmishers get shot and soon their forced to return after losing too many soldiers. More skirmishers are sent out in greater numbers and the scouts are slowly forced back.

The feds clearly didn't notice that the scouts made sure to use a very specific route. They learn the hard way when one of the skirmishers is blown to bits. After that they all freeze, easy targets for the scouts who now turned to fire their remaining ammunition into the skirmishers. Again they are forced to withdraw, this time much slower. The confederate army breaks up and begins sending out units to clear the mines.

With the scouts low on ammo I give the order for squads to leave the safety of the fort to make the minesweepers work harder. When the first of them gets shot the rest quickly break. Can't blame them, not many people could disarm a mine while being shot at. I certainly wouldn't want to be in their shoes.

The feds seem unfazed and begin setting camp. They were now close enough that I could see individuals set up their tents. Man what I wouldn't do for some artillery right now. All those soldiers in close proximity… Damn I wish i'd brought some motors at the very least. I may have been able to really bloody them. Not seeing any point in watching anymore I leave the window. Heading downstairs I find a couch and lay on it. One of the benefits of command is I can sleep while others fight. Now if only I could.

8/20/1441
0600

Artillery shells fall on the fertile farmland, turning the ground to a smoldering crater. A direct path is made through the minefield all the way to the base of the hill. A few stray shots slam into the hill but nothing comes close to the main buildings where my unit waited. This bombardment repeats on all four sides until nothing is left of the fertile plains but craters. Not only had they cleared the mines they have also provided cover for their soldiers to use when they advance.

At least that's probably what the enemy commander is thinking. Even without getting on the rooftops we have clear lines of sight inside most of the craters. If they think those craters will serve as anything more than their graves they'll have a rude awakening. Even should they get to the relative safety at the base of the hill we'll just start lobbing grenades. Even without using the grenade launcher attachment the shrapnel grenades should prove devastating to those climbing the hill.

My only real concern is supplies. We only have a month's worth of food, not counting the food the townspeople had left behind. In terms of ammo we had thousands of rounds for the machine guns but those will go quickly. For our rifles we brought a thousand rounds and five HE grenades. Everyone also has another five shrapnel and smoke. Command had expressed concerns about whether we'd be able to arrive on time but they clearly didn't know how we train. Back at basic we each would of been carrying a machine gun on top of the ammo and food.

Seeing some movement from the enemy ranks draws my attention. Scanning their movements I can't help but sigh. It would appear that more soldiers are coming in. Divisions were moving in the sections of their lines that I could see and it wouldn't be a strength to assume the same thing is happening all around. If they were sending this much after us than they have recognised the importance of the hill. It also means they are planning to fight here.

On one hand I should be happy that they committed so many troops to what is essentially a distraction. Of course that also means that I may not be able to hold this hill. Bullets are great and all but no amount of them can help you against artillery. If they want they can level this hill.

Now if they did that they'd claim the hill but they'd ruin it strategically for the upcoming battle. A hill with nothing but craters at the top is not suitable for the big guns. Take into account how how much they'll be wanting every shell when the Alliance shows up. For both of those reasons I am not diving into the towns well for cover or contemplating my impending demise.

This was an opportunity that my duty demands that I exploit. So long as they don't decide to level the hill I have the chance to bleed the enemy a bit. A major battle will be fought here within the week so any resources they use on us they can't use to win the important battle. Is this what command is? Deciding when the lives of your men are to be sacrificed for the greater picture. If I get the chance i'll have to ask Steel about it.

The feds take me out of my thoughts again when they start sending out platoon sized units. While their marching their artillery shoots out shells filled with smoke to mask their infantries movement but I know this is all just a test. Their commander is sending small units to their death so that he can figure out where the best place to strike is.

The smoke blinds us but we don't mind. It just means they'll be closer when we can shoot them. Sure enough when they appear from the smoke their gunned down by rifle fire. I'd made it clear I didn't want to use machine guns if we could avoid it. No reason to waste such a valuable resource, especially when the enemy can be dispatched with rifles. After no more than an hour the few survivors disappear back into the smoke. Behind them they leave a hundred or so of their comrades.

A couple hours pass before the another larger enemy force marches out to assault us. Again and again they send out probing forces and again and again they leave with a fraction of their numbers. By the time the sun starts to go down I count no fewer than a thousand dead in the section I was watching. Every soldier dead is a small victory, every bullet they lose is a tragedy. Those soldiers dead in the dirt have a lot of bullets the enemy will be wanting sooner or later. Hopefully thing will keep going like this.

8/21/1441
0000

The roar of machine guns fill the air with such a sound that if I didn't have earplugs i'm confident i'd have lost my hearing. Even in training i've never heard so many guns going off at one time. Considering i'm fairly safe behind the main lines in a house I have to wonder what it's like for the thousands of soldiers assaulting our position. They must be terrified, the air filled with bullets and knowing that they couldn't retaliate. In that light my unit is doing them a service by ending their pain.

Not sure if the feds are thinking the same thought but considering the ever increasing pile of bodies at the base of the hill I wonder if they even care. How many of their soldiers have died so far? Five thousand? Ten? I'd have ordered this place leveled once the the dead reached four digits and yet some of my squad leaders estimate over ten-thousand confederate soldiers are spread out all over the area around the hill. Some of them are concerned that they'll be able to use their dead as a ramp if this continues.

Taking a sip out of my canteen I take a moment to try and figure out how they'll try and push us off our hill. Sooner or later they'll reach a limit to the number of dead they can accept. When that happens they'll have to get smarter if they want to take this hill. Going downstairs I head to the dining room where the table now has a detailed map of the area and on a chair a radio for me to contact command. I ignore the radio and instead focus on the map.

The landscape has changed considerably since this map was made. The surrounding area now had craters all around the hill and now mounds of not just dirt but corpses. There was no way we could even hope for a detailed map but it's better than nothing. To help keep the map up to date the two reserve squads are acting as runners. Even as I think about it, one of them heads into the room and nods to me. After I nod back he goes over to the map and takes out a pencil and erases a enemy division. After he's thoroughly removed the mark he makes a new one near my sector.

"They're concentrating their forces." The man seems to take my statement as a question and nods.
"Yes sir. I ran into a couple of the others and their saying the same thing. Whole divisions converging." I nod and look over the defences we'd worked so hard to set up.
The walls and barricades wouldn't hold out against a prolonged assault. For now they made great cover and kept the enemy from knowing our resources but if they got at the gates they'd be able to tear them down. Whoever is in charge over there must of realized that if their preparing for a concentrated assault. They are probably hoping to break our lines with sheer numbers. Looking over to the man finishing up with the map I form a plan.

"Gather your squad and tell them to come to my sector. Inform the other squad their to take up position here. I want them to be able to rush to any sector of the line in a moments notice." He straightens up and puts away his pencil.
"Right away sir!" He darts out of the room with a smile on his face. No doubt he's grown tired of being a runner and is looking forward to the action. Looking at the marks that indicated the enemy divisions we know about I smile myself. If nothing else it'll be a battle for the history books.

8/21/1441
0540

Looking out the window I flinch back as a bullet flies past where my head was a moment before. The roar of explosions tell me that they've gotten to the base of the hill. It won't be long before they start storming up. With that in mind I throw one of my own shrapnel grenades. A couple seconds later the explosion goes off and even over the machine guns I hear the cries of pain from soldiers who were just pelted by shrapnel.

Before I can can get to full of myself I feel the shockwave of a large explosion. Soon after I hear shouts and know that they've breached one of the walls. Heading out of the room i'd been using as a sniper's perch I make my way to ground level. Once there I open the door to the main street and immediately the door is riddled with rifle fire.

A grenade goes off in the distance and for a moment i'm left alone. I lean out of the doorway and see several confederate soldiers pouring through a breach in the improvised wall. Some of them move to enter the nearest buildings where they know some of us are firing at their comrades. The moment they make to open the door an explosion tears the intruder to bits and the others that were getting ready to breach are knocked to the ground. Me and the others that have come to contain the breach finish off the survivors.

I see a couple of feds aiming my way and duck back into the building before they pull their triggers. Taking the time to pull out another shrapnel grenade I lean out and throw it as hard as I can towards the breach. It gets just outside of the hole the feds had created before detonating. Some of the feds that had just entered fall to ground screaming in agony and I can only hope that those outside didn't fare better.

Taking up my rifle again I open fire at anyone that dares to enter. A few of them make it through and enter the buildings where their comrades had failed to gain a foothold. I can only trust that whoever is in there is able to repel their guests while I focus on the new wave of feds charging into the town. Another CA fires a high explosive grenade out of their rifle and the whole street shakes a bit as it lights up the area in a fiery explosion. Few are left alive after that blast and none live long enough to regain their footing.
Taking the time i've been given I reload. Pulling out a clip I shove it into the rifle and lean out to be met by smoke pouring in from the breach. Another grenade is fired and before it even goes off i'm extending the bayonet. The explosion blows away the smoke along with some unlucky confederate soldiers. Instead of shooting them from here I rush out and make my way into one of the buildings that the feds had invaded.

Once inside I see a fed wrestling with one of my men while another is attempting to line up a shot. I slice the riflemans leg from behind and as he falls to a knee I impale him through the back. The wrestling duo sepeartae briefly. The confederate soldier smiles, sure in his victory. He's still smiling when I put a round through his skull. I don't get time to look at my compatriot as another fed charges in. A swift parry followed by a rifle butt to the face sends the soldier to the ground where a blade insures he won't be a problem again.

Without thinking I dive out of the way of the door as two soldiers barge in. The CA who'd taken out his pistol at this point makes short work of them. They fall dead but even as they hit the floor more soldiers are beginning to pour into the building. I level my rifle and fire at the intruders, while I do my comrade pulls out two grenades and tosses them out the door. A dual explosion of smoke and shrapnel fill the street outside and the enemy's momentum is halted for the moment.

Using this time to our advantage we exit the building and make our way to the breach. I nearly collide with a woman as she rushes in. Thankfully she does most of the work and impales herself on my rifle but then she grabs it with both hands and refuses to let it go. I see some grenades hanging from her chest and reach out with my free hand and pull a pin. Not wasting a second I release my hold on my rifle and kick her out of the breach. She falls back and begins to leave my line of sight and I place my arms over my face. The explosion knocks me back and I feel my back crash into the ground.

Everything's a blur of colors. Looking at the breach I see CAs tossing grenades as fast as they can. I feel a hand grab my shoulder and look up to see someone is dragging me away from the battle. They take me into a building where another person looks into my eyes. I see their lips moving but all I hear is a dull ringing in the back of my head. A canteen is forced into my hands and I instinctively take a swig. The cold water enters my body and washes away my weariness. Everything comes into focus and I look around the room with clear eyes. I'm in a house. I need to get back in the fight.

Waving the others off they exit the building and find cover in doorways all along the main street. I drag myself over to the door and draw my pistol. Leaning out I see that the feds have taken at least the first couple houses. A few of them are trying to break down the barricades blocking off the side streets and alleys. Before they can complete their task their gunned down. No one else seems interested in finishing their work so I divert my attention to the breach in the wall.

Soldiers with red crosses were dragging the dead and wounded away. With them clearing the entry of obstacles the soldiers behind them are no doubt preparing for another assault. I look over to the others. Some of us still have rifles with ammo but it was clear that we wouldn't be holding them back with our guns alone. If the machine guns weren't still putting in work i'd order one brought up, but the only ones available are for the fallback position.

The best any of us can do is take this time to mop up those that had made it inside and scavenge what we can from the dead. Not a minute after the last confederate soldier in the town falls dead a mass of voices combine into a single roar. It's a sound that drowns out even the machine guns and fills me with adrenaline. Rising to my feet I use the doorframe as a crutch and point my pistol at the breach.

The moment the first head appears whoever had a grenade left throws them out the breach. Even as the explosions of metal cut down their ranks they continue onwards. None of them even think of stopping to shoot, instead they run up to CAs who quickly withdraw into their respective buildings. As the seemingly unending horde gets closer to me several rifles go off and the front runners fall over dead. Looking in the direction of the shoots I see the squad i'd placed in reserve in a double line formation.

The front row unloads into the enemy ranks and when they run dry the soldiers in the back move forward. The fresh soldiers take a knee and empty their own rifles at the enemy. The moment the last soldier has fired off the final round in their rifle the whole thing repeats. Over and over again they take turns mowing down the enemy until they reach the first building where a melee is taking place.

Soldiers from the rear row break off and rush to their comrades aid. The moment they do those who'd been holding the line since the beginning take their place. By the time they get to the breach only two could say they'd been in the formation from the beginning. Observing it from my position gives me pride and sorrow in equal measure. On one hand I am proud to call them brothers in arms but on the other I wish i'd had the strength to stand with them.

Even as the breach is closed I can't muster the strength to move from my position. Looking at the others as they gather the dead and grab any equipment in working order they start to go in and out of focus. Holding my head with one hand I slowly put my pistol away. I have clearly suffered a concussion, that or I somehow got drunk. Taking slow breaths I try and disperse the fog that was forming in my mind. A man comes up to me and breaks my concentration.

"Sir. We got command on the radio for you." I stare at him for a second before nodding.
"That's right...I'm in charge aren't I?" The man gets a confused look on his face but before he can say anything he's forced to catch me when I fail to walk.
"Sir! Are you injured?" I look at the man whose face is now inches from mine.
"Probably. Now get me to that radio!" He puts one of my arms over his shoulder and half walks me half drags me to the building I vaguely remember as being important. The

man brings me to a table with a map on it and sits me down. While I look at the map he goes over to a radio and begins fiddling with it. After a bit he hands me a handset, while he puts on a headset.

"This is...Captain Green. How may I help you?" The voice on the other line seems to fill with concern.
"Captain Green are you alright? You sound a little out of it." Squeezing my eyes shut I rub my forehead but the fog stays, through it seems to be clearing up.
"Yeah...Yeah i'm fine. Just took a hit to the head is all." The voice takes a moment before responding, no doubt wondering if I really was alright.
"Very well. We've recently received new intel from Steamburg. They report a drastic drop in the number of divisions in their area of operations. With their AO beginning to clear up they decided to attempt a breakthrough last night." The voice pauses before continuing. After a moment he starts back up again. "Today they reported that they have not only made a breakout but they managed to drive the confederate forces off. With their success and the reports we've received from you we estimate that most of the confederate army on the island is converging on your position."

I look over to the map on the table. My mind is now mostly clear with some memories being a bit hazy, but I can get a rough idea of what the feds are up to. They must have realized we were trying to pincer them. That would explain why so many divisions are currently surrounding this damn hill and why command is probably going to be telling me some really bad news. Command hadn't planned for a major engagement with a force of equal or greater strength than their own. They had planned to fight a force that was at most the same size as them.

"With this new intelligence it has been decide that more divisions and artillery support will be needed to conduct the operation. You are advised to attempt a breakout and rejoin our lines as soon as possible." My grip on the handset tightens until I worry that I may shatter it.

"As i'm sure you know a breakout is not possible. We are completely surrounded and outgunned. Without support we'll be in trouble." The voice which at one point had concern is now filled with a tone that is as cold as ice.

"We are unable to provide any support at this time. If a breakout is impossible then your only option is to hold until we are able to relief you." Looking at the map I imgien the enemy markers growing in number before they finally overwhelm the hill.

"How long until we can expect to get support." The man on the other end takes his time before answering.

"We estimate we'll be ready to engage the beginning of next month." Take in the time for them to arrive it'll be lose to two weeks before we get any help. Of course that's also assuming that things go as command plans.

"Understood command. Will hold until relieved." I pass the handset back to the man and slowly get to my feet.

"Your from Juliett right?" He nods. "Good. Get back to your squad and switch out with whoever took the greater losses. Inform them that all units on the line will be rotating like we'd planned." After a moment he heads off. Once he's gone I rub my eyes and mentally prepare myself. I need to get it together if I want to be of any help.

8/24/1441

0830

Slashing out I cut my attacker off at the knees. The woman falls back and another takes her place. Before they can get to comfortable I give their chest a solid kick that sends them into another of their comrades. A bullet brush past my head so close I can feel the heat as it passes. Turning I whip out my pistol and fire at my attacker. The man falls back but before he even hits the ground i'm parrying a blade from another soldier.

Shifting my feet a bit I parry another thrust and counter by sweeping his feet out from under him. The moment his back hits the dirt I impale him through the gut with my sword. The next squad through the breach sees this display and falter. Standing in the breach they block their allies from coming forward and leave themselves in the open. A rifle grenade impacts at their leader's feet and the whole squad is blown away.

Their comrades rush forward to avenge them but a whistle signals their doom. I quickly get out of the street and huddle in a building. Leaning out I see the feds pour through like a tidal wave. Many of them have faces filled with awe at the sight of their enemies withdrawing. Their optimism is quickly replaced with horor when they notice the machine gun at the end of the street. The ones that see the threat try to warn those behind them but before anything can be done the roar of the machine guns signals their demise. Everyone in the street is cut to ribbons as the machine gun mows them down. In less than a minute a whole company of soldiers lie dead in the street of this once peaceful town.

Turning away from the street I look into the building. The

sight and stench of the dead threatened to overwhelm my senses. Taking slow deep breaths I stop the rising feeling of disgust. This was no longer a battlefield, now it was just a butchering field and I have to wonder how the feds can stand the growing bill. They have to have lost thousands of soldiers trying to take this hill, hell I wouldn't be surprised to hear that their casualties have passed into the five digit numbers.

A woman that I recognise from alpha comes up to me. She sits opposite me and points her rifle at the breach before talking to me.
"Sir. Alpha one reports their breach closed. We took some wounded but no dead yet." I reach for a dead man nearby and drag him close. Taking his rifle and any ammo for it I look over to woman.
"Good job. Take the wounded to the fall back line and keep up the good work." She nods and gets up to leave. Before she goes the feds appear from the breach and she fires at them while withdrawing.

Taking aim with my new rifle I shoot a man through the head. While he falls to the ground I shoot another in the neck. They fall clutching at their wound and another soldier starts dragging them away. Ignoring the wounded I shoot another in the shoulder and again their dragged out of harm's way by one of their comrades. Even though I wasn't killing most of my targets I was getting more soldiers out of the fight and that's what's important at the moment.

Several shots ping off the side of the building i'm using as cover. While I withdraw behind cover another CA pops out and takes over my work. Soon he is forced to retreat out of the line of fire and I go back to work. Most of my shots are aimed towards wounding my targets but every now and again

I kill one out of habit. I can only hope that the number of wounded overwhelms the enemy and forces them to withdraw or at least take a break. If nothing else than seeing so many wounded should diminish their moral a bit.

A white flag appears from the breach. All of us lower our weapons and after a little bit a squad of unarmed soldiers with red crosses on their helmets and shoulders. One of them also wears a lieutenant's insignia and they call out for the ranking officer. Dropping my rifle I get up and dust myself off.

"What can I do for you doc?" He looks around at all the dead and wounded.
"I don't suppose you could end the war?" I shake my head.
"Well if you can't end the war then i'll just thank you for your men's restraint. Command was worried you'd be too busy to look out for the cross." Looking at the bright red cross on his shoulder I wonder how anyone couldn't notice it. Even if they didn't have eyes on their shoulder than they could easily see the one on the front and back of their helmet.
"We try not to commit too many war crimes. Now I don't think you'd call me out just to compliment me, so what do you want?" He shrugs and pulls out a letter from his back pocket.
"I was asked to give this to you. It's from the big guy himself." Looking at the letter I do see a familiar wax seal.
"Thanks. You'll forgive me if I hope I don't see you anytime soon." He smiles and extends his hand.
"Wouldn't want to see you too soon either. If you don't mind me asking… What's your name?" Can't hurt to give the man a proper introduction.
"Captain Green at your service. Sorry in advance for the work we'll be sending your way." He grimaces a moment

before letting my hand go.
"Better I have work during a battle than not, means lives may be saved."

After that he heads over to his men and they begin clearing away the dead and searching for any wounded. Judging by the lack of noise i'd guess a similar scene is playing out all over the line. With the time they give me I head into a building that I imgen used to be a lovely shoemakers shop and take a seat. After I get comfortable I open the letter and begin reading.

To the enemy commander,

As i'm sure you're aware you are not only heavily outnumbered but also outgunned. While you may be emboldened by your ability to hold us back this long i'm sure you must realize that sooner or later your lines will crumble. When that happens most of your command will no doubt perish and I for one would mourn at the loss of such valiant warriors.

No one can say that you haven't done your duty nor can anyone say that they could of done better. For the sake of everyone under your command I ask that you surrender. I swear on my honor and that of the Confederation you will be treated fairly in accordance to the laws of war. There is no shame in surrender.

Yours truly,
General Barkly IV

I almost tear the letter up but think better of it. Turning it over I take out my pencil and start writing my reply.

To enemy,

I'm happy to hear that you've been impressed by our action on the field of battle. It is unfortunate that I must inform you that we will not surrender. To be frank I don't know why you even bothered to extend such an offer so quickly. We still have plenty of munitions and even should those go dry than we have more than enough steel to go around.

In short I see no reason to end the fighting at this moment. Of course should you wish to surrender I would graciously accept. After all… There is no shame in surrender is there?

Your enemy,
Captain Green

My letters are sloppy and some words are certainly misspelled, but i'm in a hurry. Rushing out of the the shop I find one of the confederate medics and hand him the letter with a smile.
"That for your commander. Make sure he gets it as soon as possible." He nods and pockets the letter, then he gets back to work searching for any wounded among the dead.

My letter delivered I look out towards the enemy lines. I can't say if their letters has angered me or brought me some measure of joy. Regardless I now have a secounded wind and can't wait for the next assault.

8/28/1441
1400

Looking through my binoculars I see the units moving

around like mad men. Bravo two had mentioned a big shift in the enemy lines in her sector and i'd come personally to get a look. The feds were scrambling around to reform their lines in the oddest of formation that simply cannot imagine the purpose of. They seem to be parting their ranks to make a avenue for artillery to cross but from the glint of medals and number of fancy hats it appear that a large number of these men were officers.

Unlike the soldiers behind these officers who are caked in mud the officers could easily be distinguished by their clean red uniforms with golden frills and other such nonsense. Many of them had shiny medals they wore proudly on their chests. Do they realize that they were making themselves so noticeable that i'm tempted to send out skirmishers?

"I think I know what their up to." I look over to Bravo two and see her staring out her own binoculars.
"Besides making themselves a target I can't see any reason for their formation." Her smile reminds me of when a parent is explaining something to their kids.
"Their getting into parade formation. If I had to guess they were about to have an important guest come through." I look again through the binoculars and then grin.
"May I borrow your rifle sargent?" Without a word she passes me her rifle and I put my binoculars. Maxing out the scopes sights I lay down and prop the butt of the rifle on my shoulder.
"Can the mark III even reach that far?" My lips curl into a cruel grin.
"What's the range, a kilometer or so? Just need to account for gravity and wind and it should hit the target." She turns and stares through her binoculars for a moment.
"Just shy of twenty-five hundred meters. You do know that

even the generous estimates say the rifle can reach a killimer right?" I ignore her and focus on the enemy.

"Just let me know when you see someone important."

Now they had finished forming their 'parade' formation. Some of them stiffen and even this far off I can hear the faint sounds of drums. These crazy bastards really are throwing a parade.

"Man on horseback. Got some knights with him." Knights… Well that makes things interesting.

"So they've decided to throw the heavy units at us. Get someone to let the other squads to send two people each over here." She gets up and heads off. While she does I move the rifle to see the knights.

Five of them in colorful armor are marching behind a equally colorful man on horseback. He wore the red coat of the Confederation's military but had enough medals and frills that the red was obscured. Evan from so far away I can make out the medals on his chest. Every one of them is carrying a banner of their families crest on their back.

I'm sure to the soldiers that have been fighting in the mud for some time now find the sight of them to be awe inspiring. As far as i'm concerned they're an eyesore. Just looking at the mix of color they have on display makes my head hurt. I guess I should be thankful that their so easy to spot. We shouldn't have to worry about finding them on the battlefield, and when they fall they'll do so in full sight of their allies.

We'll have to concentrate our fire on them of course but they'll stand out even among their own. It's a shame taking them down will expend so much ammunition, but we can't just let them in. If they get into short… Short range. Looking closer at them I try to see of they have any ranged weapons but I don't see any. Two of them have tower shields but that's all.

"Sir the words out. Which do you want to target first?" Standing up I hand her back her rifle and smile.
"None. Focus fire on the general infantry and leave the knights to me." She quirks her head a bit but doesn't say anything. Heading out of the room I look forward to the upcoming battle. If things go to plan we'll give them more than just a bloody nose.

1522

Looking out of the breach they had worked so hard to make I can see the knights quickly outpacing their supporting infantry. The infantry had expected the knights to soak up a bit of the fire and now they found themselves the main targets. While their support dies in mass the knights continue their march at a steady pace. Their banners show their location even when they get to the base of the hill.

Standing at the breach I wait for them. It takes them several minutes which considering they were marching up a steep hill in heavy plate is pretty fast. When the first of them gets into view it's a knight in bright blue and green. They draw a great sword and leave their comrades behind to charge at me. His eagerness for first blood combined with his early attack makes him predictable. He'll be easy.

When the knight gets to me I effortlessly dodge his swing. Stepping to his side I draw gear's pistol and jam it into his armpit. When I pull the trigger the family boom is followed by the shattering of bone and metal alike. The knight falls on his chest and begins forming a large pool of blood. His comrades stop dead in their tracks. Another mistake I won't let them recover from.

I close the distance between us in an instant. One of the knights with the tower shield reacts quickly and moves in front of his comrades. Unfortunately for him his friends don't react quickly enough. Slipping past his guard I take ot a knife with my free hand and jam it into the gap behind his knees. He howls in pain and falls prone. Taking a bullet from my wrist I put it in the pistol and fire a round into his skull.

Even as his head explodes from the force of the gun I turn to see the remaining three knights. A knight in a bright red with gold stripes musters his courageous and goes to charge me but the other two stop him.

"Steel your anger Alden. We need to fight him together." The red knight looks at the speaker and shrugs them off. He yells loud enough to dim even the machine guns but like the first knight his attack is one of brute strength and not skill. It didn't help him that by the time he'd finished his swing I already reloaded. His swing is so simple that dodging the enchanted blade is as simple as breathing. Just like i'd done to the first knight I step into their blind spot and place the gun an inch away from their side.

His battle cry ends in a gurgle as the bullet tears his insides apart. As he falls to the ground I reload and look out to the horizon. Their infantry support had withstood a storm of bullets but seeing three of their most elite warriors slain is too much for them. Even as the last two knights prepare to fight me their allies abandon them. In another time or place i'd feel pity for their circumstances, but at the moment all I can do is my duty.

The shield knight draws a shortsword and places it to the side of the shield. In this stance he'll be able to strike at me if I come at from the left or straight ahead. It was a solid defensive stance, doubly so if you have someone covering your exposed flank. With his friend at their side they didn't have to worry about being outflanked. Speaking of his friend I can't help but wonder about their abilities.

The knight's armor is a darker tint of green with a bright golden trim. Compared to the rest their armor is the least colorful and unlike the others the only accessory to their armor is their banner. I hadn't cared about the other knight's house but this one interest me for some reason. The banner is two swords intercrossed over a shield. Like the banner would indicate this knight wields two swords. One a long thin blade that resembled a longsword, the other a shorter and more thinker.

The shield knight's stance can be hard to deal with but i've never heard a knight wielding swords such as these. The only dual wielding knights I can think of is the ones in legend that went into battle with great axes. But this knight is clearly different from the ones coming to mind. Their stance was that of a coiled spring and their weapons that of a duelist. This one is dangerous.

Walking back I put away my pistol. When I get to the first knight i'd killed I reach down and grab their sword. Taking a couple experimental swings I get used to the weight. The sword is top quality and along the blade I could see the enchantments glowing softly. Looking over to the knights I make my way towards them and flash them a smile.

The moment I get close the green knight goes into action. Their fast and while I manage to parry the main blade their dagger slices my left arm. Jumping back i'm nearly knocked senseless when the shield knight attempts to run me over. Sliding to their right I see an opening and stab towards their exposed sword arm. The sword cuts through their armor with the aid of the enchantments on the blade, and their arm falls limp.

Before I can finish the job the green knight blocks my killing blow and drives me off with a rapid series of attacks. After i'm forced away from their companion they glance towards them. The other knight nods and they resume their defensive formation. Looking at my arm I see my blood flowing freely, I wasn't in danger of bleeding out just yet but I really should get it looked at.

From the corner of my eye I see bravo team watching our fight. They won't help, I had told them not to in order to conserve our strength. Looking back at the knights I see the green one flicking their wrist and a flash of metal. Falling to a knee I feel the dagger grase my cheek. The knights charge and I stay kneeling until the green one swings their sword. Once the green one is mid-swing and the shield knight moving to ram into me.

Putting all my strength into a single lunge I slash the green knight across the side and then spin on my heels and draw my pistol on their comrade. Firing the pistol into their chest they fall back from the force of the blast. Turning to the green knight I'm nearly knocked over from the force of their swing. They lose all sense of skill and instead swing as hard and fast as they can. After the seventh strike my arm feels numb and I know this can't go on.

With a great deal of effort I manage to lock our blades and shove against them. Both of us glare into each other's eyes and I see a mix of anger, sorrow, and regret. They try and force me away but I keep us locked together. My wound is bad but i'm willing to bet theirs is worse. Slowly but surely their struggles die down as do my own. Soon we both step away breathing heavily. Their armor now had a red hue below the waist and down their right leg.

Falling to a knee I look over to the green knight. How cruel the world is, to nearly die to a knight with the color of my namesake. With no small amount of effort I stand back up but the green knight is unable to. They try and lunge at me but all they manage is to fall on their chest. Staring at them I admire their tenacity. Walking back to my unit I wonder if they'll live long enough for a medic to see to them. Stumbling past the breach I stop thinking about the the knight and focus on finding a medic and getting some rest.

9/04/1441
1200

Walking over the wounded I wonder if this is the end. We've run out of ammo. The outer wall has so many holes in it can't really be called a wall anymore. Confederate soldiers now hold most of the town. All we have left is our fallback line around the town well.

Around the well lay our dead and wounded. Blessedly few have fought their last battle here but far too many are too injured to fight. The barricades around the market square is made up of carts and any other material we could get. The ground around the barricade is caked in dried blood. Spent casings had formed piles that could be used to see where the thickest of fighting had taken place.

Passing alpha one I glance at the bloody bandages all over his body. Considering a grenade played a role in his injuries i'd say he looks alright. Moving to the line I count the few soldiers left able to fight. Besides myself only twelve of us remain capable of battle. No one says a word while the feds move up and form ranks.

We huddle behind whatever cover we can as they fire volley after volley into our positions. Bullets rip through thin wooden boards while the thinker carts protect us from harm. Someone cries out and curses. More bullets tear our cover to shreds. A bullet passes through my side but I barely notice it. My body is too tired to register pain. Finally after two more cries of pain the feds stop firing. The sound of boots approach us and before I leap over the barricade I look over to where the remains of my CA class. I give them a smile and head over the barricade to battle.

The lines of soldiers weren't expecting a charge and we get in their line before they know it. Swords slash out and more blood spills onto the ground. In under a minute we've killed most of the soldiers up front and for a brief moment the idea enters my head that we may pull this off. Then a bullet rips through my leg and I go to the ground. A foolish soldier comes up to finish me off and I grab their rifle with my free hand. The sword i'd taken from the knight goes through their gut and I shove him in the way of incoming bullets.

Grabbing the man's side arm I unload into a squad of soldiers. Soldiers fall over dead and more of them charge at us. I watch as a member of delta team does a similar action before a fed comes up and clubs them in the side of the head. I'd help him but my leg seems unable to hold my weight. Using my sword as a crutch I stand up. A fed runs up and I fall to the side in a slash that nearly cuts the woman in half.

Looking around me I see we are hopelessly surrounded. Rifles are aimed at us and there is no chance for us to close the distance. Only four of us are 'standing'. The feds look at us as if expecting something. After a minute of staring at us an officer looks around.

"Well. Raise your hands." Stabbing the sword into the ground. The rifles turn to point in my direction.

"Your welcome to raise them." The soldiers all glance at each other and the officer shakes his head in confusion.

"The battles over. Just surrender already." Looking at the others I shrug.

"There's only two ways this battle ends. Either you leave or we die." The soldiers back off. Glancing behind me I see everyone that can stand is slowly making their way to the front.

Covered in bloody wounds my unit raised as if from the dead to draw swords. Understandably this seems to rattle the feds. Even the officer seems to have sweat breaking out on their forehead. Rifles wave and shake, then a man drops his gun and runs. One by one follow him until the officer stands alone. With the last ounce of my strength I raise my sword and point at the man. The others follow my example and he raises his head high and salutes before turning around and walking off. Once he's gone we all slump to the ground. These is no more fight left in us. We have given our all and if they come back it'll be the end.

Chapter 24
War News

Pearl's Fate Decided In Major Battle!

The task force sent to relieve Pearl clashed with a large confederate army on the sixth. Both armies clashed in front of the town Holden which is located on top of a hill dominating the surrounding countryside. Though the Alliance task force came on the sixth the battle started much earlier.

Last month on the eighteenth, the fifth company of the twenty first regiment of Blade's elite Combined Arms started the battle. They entered Holden and evacuated the locals to safety before turning the small town into a fortress. When the confederate army came on the nineteenth they found the alliance dug in on top of the hill. What followed was countless assaults by confederate forces repelled every time by the heroic efforts of the defenders.

The confederate forces didn't let up until the full might of the Alliance entered the battle. Both sides then fought a brutal battle in the open plains. Heavy losses were taken by both armies but in the end confederate forces were routed. When alliance personal overran the enemy command tent they found records of the siege of Holder. Over ten thousand confederate soldiers died attempting to take the hill, another sixteen thousand wounded. Combining those numbers with the loses they took fighting the alliance's main army and they lost over fifty thousand soldiers. The alliance on the other hand lossed less than twenty thousand. After such a devastating defeat the feds began conducting an organized retreat. For the last week they have been sighted leaving the island under heavy naval escort.

Major naval victory at the border!

Just last week on the twenty-third a squadron from Water and Blade located and destroyed a confederate convoy! The official report reads that the convoy was made up of twenty troop transports, ten supply ships, and a escort of destroyers and cruisers. By the time the smoke cleared the escorts were sinking to the bottom along with most of the transport ships. To top it all off the squadron from Blade were able to capture all ten of the supply ships.

The loss of life on top of the supplies captured combine to make this perhaps the most costly defeat the Confederation has ever suffered at sea. Some officials have even claimed that this is the beginning of the end. One ship captain was quoted saying "The seas belong to us now!"

Kriegsland

With the Imperium in the middle of a civil war questions have been raised about Kriegsland. Mainly who is in charge of the imperial portion. Some council members have expressed interest in securing territory in the name of security. One member was quoted saying "The imperial citizens on Kriegsland need protection in these dark times. The Alliance can offer this and more."

The king of Blade had other things to say about Kriegsland however. In an official missive to the council he made it clear that all imperial claims on Kriegsland are held by princess Mary of the imperial royal family. Blade will protect her claims until otherwise stated.

ABOUT THE AUTHOR

Currently working a part time job while going to college to become a high school history teacher Drew's yet to experience what life has to offer and hopes to see the world. Drew is the second oldest of six and loves all his siblings dispite how much they may annoy him at times.

www.ingramcontent.com/pod-product-compliance
Lightning Source LLC
Chambersburg PA
CBHW051445050726
47593CB00005B/1934